CUTTER'S CROSSING

DELBERT WILLCUTT

PAGE PUBLISHING, INC.
New York, NY

First originally published by Page Publishing, Inc. 2017

ISBN 978-1-63568-394-3 (Paperback)
ISBN 978-1-63568-395-0 (Digital)

Printed in the United States of America

CONTENTS

INTRODUCTION

This story is about an old man and his wife that lived on a small farm near a small town in central Arkansas. This was in some of the best farmland in the South. Fred and his wife Annie raised their children up, and they moved off to start their own life. This left them alone to run their farm by their self.

This was in the late 1950s; it was a different time, and people worked and cared about each other and helped one another. Fred and Annie had a visit from their grandsons who stayed with them all summer to help them out. This was a very common thing for families to do in this time. This gave the children a chance to see where their roots were, and where they came from.

These two boys, Troy and Roy, were being raised in the city so the parents wanted them to know what it was like being raised on a farm. These two boys have done a lot of growing in just this short three months. They met a lot of interesting people and family. Read this story and see how this works for this family in this small town.

CHAPTER 1

MEETING AT THE COUNTRY STORE

8-12-12

Once there was a man name Fred. He was a farmer who worked very hard on a small farm, in Flat Rock County. Fred lived on this small farm with his wife, Annie; they counted on each other for everything. They could not get everything done if they did not work together as well as they did. They loved their life, and loved taking care of all their animals.

Fred's favorite was an old horse named Dobbin and a dog; his name was just plain old Dog.

Annie's favorite was a Jersey milk cow named Bessie and some Rhode Island Red chickens; they laid big brown eggs. She said they were the best for baking; with those eggs they would make anything taste good. Fred was very well known all around the valley and the small town named Cutter's Crossing by everyone, for his peanuts and water-melons that he grew each year. It had been a long year, and he was glad that everything was finished, put up, and sold for the year. This had been a great year for the all farmers in the valley. Everyone's crops were the best they have had in many years.

This will happen once in a while; this is what makes farmers do what they do from year to year. When they work the ground good and loose, get everything just right, and then spend money on seed to plant in the ground. Never knowing what kind of year they will have, if it will rain, a little, a lot, or any at all. Will it be to hot and dry or to cool and wet? Everything matters when it comes to farming.

This was in the early fifties in a rural area near the small town called Cutter's Crossing and everyone knew everyone. Farmers had to pay close attention on what and how they were doing things. It was not just them and their families that counted on whether they would eat through the winter or not. But the animals depended on whether or not they would eat through the winter. So when they would plant anything they would check with the farmer's almanac; that was their planting guide. It would tell you what the weather was going to be for the whole year. It had a planting schedule that was set up by the parts of your body. You always wanted to check your signs before you plant. You never wanted to plant anything when the signs were in a vital part of your body or any of your internal organs, like the heart, liver, but the arms, legs, hands were pretty much OK. Now if you wonder what farmers do in the fall and winter, when everything has been done, well I will tell you. Most all farmers have animals they raise for food like chickens, pigs, and beef cows. So they take care of those though the winter. But when all the feeding is done, this is a time to fix and repair anything that has broken that they didn't have time to work on when it broke. Some farmers like to hunt deer and small game, hunt rabbit, squirrel, dove, and pheasant. When they were not doing that, they just like hanging out in a local spot in town where they could meet. They would sit and talk about anything they could think of. They would drink coffee cup after cup; if anyone asked them what they are doing every day, they say the same thing, that they are solving all the worlds' problems.

This was one day round the first week in November. It was a clear sunny day but it was cool. Fred got up and had everything done up early. Annie knew what Fred was up to. Annie, she knew him pretty well, and she had been married to him for forty-eight years.

So Fred asked Annie if she needed anything from Polly's market. Annie said, "No, but don't go down there and stay all day. Fred went out to the barn to call Dobbin up his old workhorse." He never learned how drive; this wasn't uncommon in those days for someone not to drive an automobile. So he would hook Dobbin up to a rubber-wheeled wagon. Dobbin was already up in the lot just outside of the barnyard. Fred said, "Let's go to town." Dobbin was always ready to go to town. So he came running to the barn. Fred got him all hooked up to the wagon and called for Dog. "If you want to go to town you better come on. Dobbin and I are about to leave," Fred said.

Well, Fred didn't see Dog anywhere, but he would always catch up before they would leave the driveway. Sure enough Dog came running up across the yard, jumped up in the back of the wagon. Fred said, "You liked to have got left now sit down and be still."

CHAPTER 2

HANGING OUT AT POLLY'S

Fred thought he would stop by Frank's house to see if he would want to ride into town. Frank was the town handyman. That man could fix anything. Everyone all over the valley would bring him things to work on. Sometimes he would be so busy working on other people's things, he would hardly have time to fix his own things. That Frank, he would not tell anyone if he didn't have the time to help them with what they needed. Somehow he could always get around to doing or fixing whatever they needed. He was a good and kind man and always wanted to help anyone if they needed it. He was a tall, middle-aged man; he was a very strong and a hard worker for a man his age. When he pulled up, Frank was out front of his workshop, working on an old hay rake, putting on some new fingers where some had broke. "Why are you working on that old hay rake? It won't be time to bale hay for six months." Fred said.

"Because this is a good time to catch up on things that I have been putting off till I could get to it," said Frank. "What are you and Dog up to?"

"Well, we thought we would go to town for a bit. Do you want to come with us?" Fred asked.

"Well, maybe," said Frank,

"Do you thank Little John will be down at Polly's market?" Frank asked.

"Yes," Fred said.

"Well then yes," Frank said.

"I have not had a good laugh all day. Let's go," said Frank.

Little John was a farmer who lived out east of town on a pig farm. He did very well at it. Little John had so many stories he would tell. And if he had done everything he had said he has done, he would be at least 150 years old. But this made the time passing real enjoyable. Little John was a little round man, middle-aged, around his sixties. All the hair he had on his head was a small patch around his ears and the back of his head. He never wore a hat because when he did the slightest breeze would blow it off. He said he got tired of chasing it and picking it up. That's why he didn't wear a hat; his head was so shiny and slick that he never could find a hat that would stay on even if the wind wasn't blowing—the hat would just slide right off. And the top of his head was always cut or scratched. He was always hitting it on something in his hog house. And he would always have a long tale on how it happened. He always had on a pair of overalls; they were the striped ones like the engineers wore. Everyone liked Little John; he was a good and caring person, and you could always count on him to help out anyone that need his help.

CHAPTER 3

LITTLE JOHN'S TALL TALES

When we got to Polly's, we saw that some of the guys were already there. We went in; they were sitting around a big potbelly stove.

John the county agent said, "Before you two sit down, you have to go out and get more wood for the fire."

John didn't have much to do, now that all the farming was done for the winter. So he would help the local farmers work on their farm plan for the coming year. Of course the farmers pretty much knew what they would plant. They had been farming before he was even born. But they would let him think he was doing a good job and whatever he said was very important.

I think John learned more from the farmers around the valley in the past ten years than when he had been the county agent. Than he would have learned in fourteen years at the university out of the books they gave him to learn from. John was the type that whatever you needed, he was always ready to jump in and help. He would just roll up his sleeves and get right in and get dirty with you. And everyone liked John and would help him when he needed it. When Fred and Frank got back with two big armloads of firewood, Fred said, "This should last a while." "Where is little John?"

"Has anyone seen him?"

Polly spoke up and said, "He hadn't been in here in the past three or four days."

"Oh my," said Frank, "when he comes in, he will be wound up like an eight-day clock."

"Polly, you make sure that you tell everyone if you see him or if you know when he would be coming in. We may as well sit down and have a soda and thick slice of Petty Jean bologna and some crackers," said Fred.

Fred and Frank went over and sat down by Joe. Frank asked how the blacksmith shop was doing. And he needed him to order some new plow point for that new three-bottom plow he got last year. Frank had gotten him a new red tractor and needed a bigger turning plow.

They finished their soda and snack and Fred said, "Well, Frank, you ready to go back home?" They got up and walked over to the door just as little John was coming in. Frank Looked at Fred and said, "Well, we may be here a while. Lets go back and set back down."

"Polly said he hadn't been in the store in three or four days," Frank told Fred.

Fred knew he would be backed up with tales, and this should be quite an interesting afternoon.

The first thing, Little John got over by the stove and backed up to warm his backside. Frank noticed he had a bandage on his head.

Poor little John's head was like a road map, had so many scars. If he would only wear a hat, when he would bang his head on something in his hog house, it might not leave a mark. About that time his pants was getting very hot from being backed up to the stove. And before he could finish his sentence, when he would get real excited, he would stutter. Well, he started stuttering and dancing a little jig. "What's wrong, Little John?"

"There's not anything wrong except it felt like my paints were on fire." Everyone got a big laugh out of that.

"Think I will just get me some coffee, maybe that will warm me up," said little John.

Joe spoke up and asked, "Where have you been?"

Joe was the type of man who would always get things started when Little John was in the store. He could always keep the stories going.

Joe said, "No one saw you for a few days."

Little John said, "Well, I have been on a short vacation."

Joe said, "Well, tell us where you went."

"I went up north to do some fishing. I have a cousin that lives up at Point Remove River. They have been catching big brown bass there."

Frank asked, "How many brown bass did you catch?"

"We caught a few, but mostly little ones. But the oddest thing happened. I was in my boat floating downstream, I wasn't catching much. I had been watching a squirrel play up on a limb that hung over the water. And about the time I got under the limb that squirrel fell down in my open tackle. That squirrel got hooks and some of my new lures all over him, and is in jumped out of the boat when he'd saw me. And he went to swing to the bank. I got to watching and looking at him, I said, 'Oh my, you never heard such splashing in your life.' So I paddled over and got my dip net to dip him out. I didn't want to see him drown. I thought a squirrel could swim. When I dipped him out of the water, I want you to know I caught two bass and three crappie from that squirrel. Then I just paddled to the bank and went home. I didn't think I could top that if I fished the rest of the day."

All the men just looked at each other and they were about to crack up.

Little John said, "That was nothing. You will never guess what happened the next day. I have been seeing some geese flying around just below my house, out by my big stock pond. I told my wife to get to boiling water and that I'll be bringing home goose for supper. I drove down there, got my truck out, and walked over to the water then slipped down the pond bank. My shotgun fell right into the water and went straight to the bottom. The water was too muddy, I couldn't see where my gun landed."

So I went to the truck and got me some string and a three-pronged hook, to see if I could snag it and pull it up.

By this time it was lunchtime, so I thought I would eat my sandwich and think about how I could get my shotgun back. When I noticed that my wife had packed me a bacon sandwich, I remember how much geese liked bacon. As soon as they eat it they pass it. So I tied a piece of bacon on the string and threw it out where they would see it, and hid in the bushes. It was not long when a big goose walked up swallowed and passed it right out, and the string went straight though him. And along came another, same thing, swallowed it and so on. After I had three on the string, I just pulled them up together, put them in a sack, and pitched them in the back of the truck. Yes we had goose for supper that night. I had to go swimming to get my shotgun out of the pond. Liked to have never got it all clean and dried out. Well, guys, I am going coon hunting tonight if my new carbide light came in. Little John walked over to talk to Polly. By that time the men were rolling and laughing on the floor.

Fred looked over at Frank and said, "We have got to get out of here and go home while we can." It was midafternoon by this time. Dog was laying up on the seat in the wagon, taking his afternoon nap.

Fred said, "Wake up, Dog, get in the back. We need to go home." Fred and Frank laughed almost all the way back home at the stories that Little John had told.

CHAPTER 4

CLARE'S ROCK THROWING

They came up on Clare Bell's house. She was a tall mid-dle-aged woman that had a farm where she lived her whole life. She was a strange German lady who always talked to her animals like they were real people. She cared a great deal for them, and said they were a part of her family. Clare's mother and father settled here in Cutter's Crossing long ago when it was only a store at a crossroad. People had started to settle in the valley and would do all their buying and trading in the local store. Dan, her old workhorse, was running up the road.

"What has got into Dan?" said Frank.

He was running really fast when he passed them. About that time Clare stepped out on the road with a handful of rocks. She had been throwing them at Dan.

Frank said, "We had better stop and help her get Dan back up in the pen before she cripples someone with those rocks."

"Why are you throwing rocks at Dan?" Frank asked.

"He keeps on opening the gate and letting Beverly the milk cow and himself out, and Beverly will be eating up what's left of the winter alfalfa hay," said Clare.

"Well, have you tried to tie the gate closed? He can't untie it. He doesn't have fingers," said Frank.

Frank walked back up the road and called to Dan. He stopped running. He was glad to hear a kind voice. So he went up to Frank and they walked back up to the house together. They started to walk back across the yard to the barn.

Clare was talking to Fred when she saw Dan. She still had some rocks left in her hand and started to throw it at Dan. Dan saw Clare wind up, and he started running again, this time to the barnyard and though the gate to the back of the lot.

Frank said, "Clare stop throwing at him. "Just tie the gate closed and he can't get out."

"That old horse needs to learn that he can't just leave the gate wide open if he's going to open it and walk out. He needs to start closing it behind him," said Clare.

Fred looked at Frank and said, "We better just leave them alone and go on home. They will work it out somehow."

They got up in the wagon and Fred took Frank on home. Frank got out at his house and thanked Fred for an exciting day.

Frank said, "Let's do this again real soon."

Fred went on home. Annie was getting ready to start the milking. When Fred and Dobbin pulled up to the barn, Annie asked Fred, "What kept you, was Little John at Polly's?"

"Yes," Fred said.

"I have some new stories to tell you. You will never believe these tales," Annie said.

"Why do all of you men sit there and listen to those lies?"

"I don't know, maybe because I sit there and laugh till my stomach hurts. I know I didn't get any work done, but that sure was a lot of fun of wasting time," Fred said.

Annie said, "Here's your bucket. Old Bessie needs milking before she bust."

"Oh all right," said Fred, he walked out to the back of the barn, and Bessie was standing at the gate ready to come in. Fred let her in. He had already put some of her favorite grain in, and he had it mixed up at the coop. It had wheat, corn, alfalfa pellets, and molasses. Fred had sat down and started milking when he heard the loudest racket coming from just out in the pigpen. He got up and ran out to see what it was. His old sow had piglets, and one had got out of the pen, and Dobbin was trying to get it to go back in the hole it came out of. Fred said, "Good luck on trying to drive a pig anywhere." Fred said, "But thanks for the help, I will take it from here." Fred chased that pig around until he could hardly stand up. Finally he ran him in the barn and caught him, carried him back and put him back with the mother. This made her happy. But by this time Bessie had eaten all of her grain and was ready to go back in the pasture for the night. And he still had not milk yet, so he set back down and finished the milking, then took the milk back to Annie. She strained the cream off the milk and put it in the icebox for the night.

CHAPTER 5

LITTLE JOHN'S PET PIG

Dog jumped up on the porch and stared barking up a storm. Annie said, "Fred, go out and see what Dog is barking at." Fred had just gotten comfortable in his favorite chair. He said, "I love my life on this farm. There is never a dull moment. It seems like something is going on all the time." By the time Fred got out on the front porch, Little John's coon dogs came running by the house, and Little Missy was right with them. She was grunting every step, and Little John right behind them hollering SOOWIE! SOOWIE! Everything went quiet when they passed, so Fred went back into the house.

Annie said, "What was all that?"

Fred said, "That was all of Little John's coon dogs, and that pet pig Missy, she was just running and grunting right along with them."

Annie said, "That is just strange and that's not natural for a pig to run after coon dogs like that."

The next day, Annie said, "Fred, will you go to town and pick up some more cornmeal? We will have sweet milk and corn bread tonight for supper." Fred got Dobbin hooked up to the wagon and off they went. Dog caught up about the time they pulled out on the road. Fred said, "Dog, sit down and be still." When they got to town, Fred went into Polly's market, and Little John had just gotten in there. He had a big burn on his head; it was all blistered up looked real bad.

Fred said, "What happen to you?"

"Well, I have to talk to Polly about that. The carbide light I picked up yesterday, I think it was defective," Little John said. "It caught my hat on fire. I don't think I will not be wearing that on my head anymore."

Polly looked at Little John's head. "That carbide light you sold me caught your hat on fire?"

"Yes it burned my head," Little John said.

Polly said, "I talked to my cousin Ralph in Kentucky. He supplies some of the coal miners' lights to use in those deep mines. He said that that was what all the coal miners use." "What kind of hat did you have on?" asked Polly.

"I was wearing my old straw hat. It had been hanging in the barn for a while. But it still fit me pretty well," Little John said.

"I would like to have my money back. I will just use my old coal oil lantern."

Polly said, "Ralph sent me some metal hard hats that you use with those carbide lights. He said they burn real bright and hot. Sorry I forgot about telling you that you need a metal hard hat to wear with it."

"Well, I won't be able to wear a hat till my head heals up anyway," Little John said.

Polly asked Little John, "Did you tree any coons?"

"After that happened, Missy and the dogs ran off ahead so for that I lost them. Didn't see them till the next day, when they came home to eat something," Little John said. "I will take one of those hats that go with the light and give it another try as soon as my head heals."

Fred picked up the cornmeal Annie wanted and went outside. John the county agent came up to Fred.

"I will need you to bring some peanuts to roast, for a meeting, with all the farmers in the area on the 12th of December. It will be our Christmas party," John said.

"You can count on it, John," said Fred. "We will be talking about building a farm plan for next year. I have a slide show I thank everyone will enjoy. I will get with you in a week or so," John said.

Fred got back to the wagon. Dog was lying on the seat, asleep. He put the cornmeal in the back, and dog woke up and was glad to see Fred. He knew it was time to go back home. It didn't take very long, and they made it back home. Fred drove out to the front of the barn and unhooked the wagon from Dobbin and turned Dobbin out in the back lot. He picked up the cornmeal and walked to the house and gave it to Annie.

Fred said, "You'll never guess what happened to Little John now."

"What happened?" Annie said.

"He set his hat on fire and burned the top of his head."

"Did he burn the rest of the hair he had on his head off?" Annie asked?

"Just about," said Fred.

"He has a big blister on the front of his head."

"Oh my, how did it happen?" Annie asked Fred.

"Polly ordered a carbide light that fits on your head for his coon hunting. He strapped it to his straw hat. It got hot and caught on fire. Polly forgot to give him the metal hard hat that comes with the head lamps. Polly said he was sure sorry."

Annie said, "Poor Little John, his head looks like a road map now, with all the scars on it."

"Well, looks like he will have one more road to add to his map on his head," said Fred.

"Oh by the way, we are having a farm meeting at John's office. It will be our Christmas party," Fred said.

"It will be a potluck meal. You need to get with Clare on what to bring. She is in charge of the food."

CHAPTER 6

FARMERS' CHRISTMAS PARTY

It was time to go to the farmers' meeting, and all the farmers looked forward to this every year. John always had a lot of useful tips for everyone to try out on their next crop. That John tries so hard to help every farmer to have the best crop they could have. John was very well liked and everyone made him feel like he had a very important job. But all the farmers, they were all set on what they were going to plant the next year.

Fred said, "I sure hope we get the rain and the warm weather we got this year for next year."

John stood up and started the meeting. Everyone had a great year. Joe Green had the best grape crop he had in years. Fred grew the biggest watermelons I have ever seen this year. And his peanuts were just great. Clare Bell's sweet potatoes, well, everyone seen her and Dan pulling them into town load after load. John said.

We all had good corn crop. "Everyone's livestock should get big and fat though the winter. We all have a lot to be thankful for this year. I am so glad that you good folks let me be your county agent here in Cutter's Crossing. You sure make my job easy. With all that said, let's say grace and eat this good food everyone brought before it gets cold."

Everyone sat down and just got started eating good when Joe Green got up and opened the front door. With all the people in John's office, it was very hot so they wanted it to cool off a little bit. They heard a loud noise. Then in came a big old bore coon and Missy right behind it and then all Little John's coon dogs behind her. Well, with all that food in there, Missy and the coon dogs forgot about the coon that he made a circle and ran right on back out. The coon dogs and Missy jumped up on the tables and started eating as fast as they could. Let me tell you, if you had not ever seen a half-starved coon dog eat, well they can suck down a lot food before you can blink an eye, and as for pigs you know how they can eat. Little John was coon hunting just outside of town; he thought the coon would head for the bottoms instead of coming into town. He could tell from the sound of his dogs where they went. So he headed into town to see what kind of damage his dogs had done. Little John pulled up outside John's office. By that time all the men had ran the dog out. But the women were very mad at little John.

Clare said, "Hey, Little John, Missy forgot her dessert."

Clare threw a sweet potato pie at Little John.

She was usually not very good at throwing things, but it was just Little John's luck that he got it right up side of the head.

Then the other ladies started throwing food at little John.

Little John got back in his truck and got out of town. All the men likely have busted a gut laughing.

Fred looked at John and said, "I think this is one of the best meetings you have ever put together."

We finally got everything cleaned up. Then we sat down watched John's slide show. John went to a lot of trouble getting all that together for us; he really had some good ideas. But getting the farmers to change the way they are used to doing things, well, John has his work cut out for him. It's all because their families and their livestock count on us to make sure that we make a crop. Big or small so that everyone has something to eat though the long and cold winter. That's why it's so hard to change, even if it does make sense.

Christmas came and went. Everyone had a wonderful time with all their family and friends. We didn't get any snow in December, but it sure was cool. All the snow came in January; it was cold and long. We had a lot of snow, and Dobbin and Bessie spent most of the time in the barn with the other animals. I had my fill of snow for one year, but that's the best thing for our ground, that slow-melting snow. It will loosen up the soil, so that all the nutrients can get in the ground. That will make everything grow good and healthy next year.

February was very cold; no one got out much except to check on neighbors. That was the good thing about living in the valley; you could always count on people helping one another. My dad always said, "Surround you and your family with good and kind and caring people. And when times are good you help those that are in need. And when times are bad they will help you. Everyone needs help sometimes. Be ready and when the time comes. Step up and help out. They will be grateful that you did. They may not ask, but even the smallest amount you can give will be a lot when they have nothing."

CHAPTER 7

FRED AND ANNIE'S SURPRISE

Fred and Annie worked very hard. They were in their sixties and getting older. Their kids had grown up and moved away, and that left Fred and Annie to work the farm. They missed having their son and daughter to help them around the farm. They had to get up earlier and work longer just to get everything done. Their daughter married a fine young man, and he got a good education at the university. Now he has a very important job in Chicago at one of those car factories, and they're doing really well. They have two sons and a daughter. The boys' names are Troy and Roy. They are not twins. Roy is ten, Troy is eight, and Lizzie is six years old.

Annie went to the mailbox one day and got a letter from Kathy and Jim, the kids' mom and dad.

Fred was out in the peanut patch, and he just finished weeding and came in for supper. Annie told Fred about the letter that they received today from the kids. So after supper Annie got the letter and opened it. Annie just burst into tears.

Fred looked at her and said, "What happened?"

Annie said that Troy and Roy want to come and stay the summer with them and learn about farm life.

This made Fred and Annie very happy. They had not gotten to see them for three years this past Thanksgiving. But they would always right letters every few weeks are so. It was always so good to hear from them; they missed all of them so much.

Fred had all the crops planted and about all he had to do was to cut weeds out of the peanuts and melons. This was the first of June, and there was not much picking to do just yet. It wasn't time for many things to be ripe. The letter said they would be staying till first of September. Fred thought this would see if they have any farmers' blood in them or not. The first of September would take us though harvest time. I sure hope those boys have grown; they were very skinny last time we've seen them. Maybe Annie could put some weight on them, they are going to need it, Fred thought. Well, this was Monday when we got the letter, and it said they would be here on Friday afternoon on the train. Kathy said they couldn't bring them; Jim couldn't get off work, and Little Lizzie was going to stay with her mother so it would just be Troy and Roy. But they would be coming up to pick the boys up and stay for a week, the first of September. Annie worked hard to get everything ready for the boys. She told everyone she knew around close, and everyone was willing to help out in any way they can. It is so good to have good neighbors that will treat you like family. And they don't even have to, just because they care.

Well, Friday afternoon finally came, and it was time for Fred and Annie to go out and hook up old Dobbin to the wagon, and off they went into town to meet the train.

They were very excited about seeing the boys. They got there early, and the train was late, so they sat out front and waited on the bench.

A little while later they heard the train coming down the tracks a long way off, but it didn't take long, and it was pulled into the depot. The boys were the first ones off the train; they were ready to see their grandparents. They have grown so much that Fred and Annie hardly even knew them, but Roy knew them right away. Roy and Troy ran over to them and grabbed Annie right away. This made Annie feel so good, she told Fred later that she thought she was going to melt with joy when she saw those two boys.

CHAPTER 8

SLOW WAGON RIDE HOME

They picked up their bags and loaded them up in the wagon. Dog was happy to see the boys. Troy asked Grandpa Fred, "Where is your car?"

"I don't have a car, I never learned to drive. Besides they go way too fast for me and Grandma Annie. This is the best way to go, it's a lot safer. A little slower, you just have to give yourself a little more time to get where you're going," Fred said. On the way home there was never a minute for anyone to catch a breath. When they pulled up at home, Annie got out at the house; they unloaded the bags and carried them into the house.

Fred said, "I will go unhook Dobbin and milk old Bessie and be right back."

The boys were ready to go out to the barn and see all the animals. They had mostly been in the city on concrete in their whole life. City life was all they knew; Fred looked at Annie and said, "We better keep a close eye on those two boys. They were too small to go out around the animals, the last time they were here. They have never even seen anyone milk a cow before. They thought that the milk came from the supermarket. Well, Fred, what do you want me to do, put some molasses on their fingers and give them a feather to play with."

"They will be just fine," Annie said. Bessie was standing at the gate and was ready to be milked so it didn't take long to fill the milk bucket. She really was letting the milk fly. A cow can hold back some of her milk if she wanted to, if they have a calf that they are suckling. I thank Bessie was just showing off for the boys.

Fred finished up milking and then turned Bessie out in the back lot. He carried the milk to the house to be strained and put in the icebox for the night

Troy asked Annie what she would do with all that milk. Would they have to drink all the milk each day?

"Oh no," Annie said. She would make butter and cheese out of some of it and take some to town to be sold at the market. By this time it was getting late, and Annie started to unpack their things and noticed that they didn't have anything to play in. They got Troy and Roy settled in to their bedroom, and Annie looked over at them, and they were already asleep. She walked out and said to Fred, "We are going to have to get them something to wear to play in. About all they brought with them were fancy clothes. They can't play anything that looks like that. We will save them to wear to Church on Sundays. They can wear the shoes that they brought with them, if they won't."

But Fred said, "They will need to learn how to go barefoot around here like the other kids around here do. That will toughen their feet up."

The next day Fred and Annie were up early, and the boys were still asleep. Annie got their breakfast ready at

7:30 a.m. Fred had everything done up outside and went in to eat with the Annie and the boys. After breakfast, Annie said, "We will go into town and pick you boys something out that you can wear to play in."

The boys were ready to go to town. But the pancakes they had for breakfast Annie made, well it took a while to fill them up. Annie looked at Fred and said, "I may have a full-time job just cooking for everyone. Those boys, they have a good appetite."

Annie had enough batter left to make Fred one more pancake, but Roy asked if he could have it.

About that time Troy finished up and went out to the barn to look for Dobbin. That's about the time Fred heard the loudest noise you ever heard coming from the pigpen. Fred jumped up and ran out to the pigpen and Roy right behind him. Troy had let all six of the piglets out, and the mother pig was having a fit. The gate to the pen was wide open, and the old sow was coming at Troy just as Fred got to the gate and closed the gate on the old sow's head and shooed her back into the pen. And now they had six little piglets running around everywhere to catch. Fred was impressed with Roy; for a ten-year-old boy he was pretty fast.

But not fast enough to catch a little pig. They finally ran them into the barn where they could catch them and put them one by one back with their mother.

Fred told Troy, "I got you this time, but boy they are two things you have to pay close attention to, and that is a big Jersey bull and a sow with piglets. They will tear you apart, I am not kidding. They are very dangerous. Please stay away from the sow. I don't want anything to happen

to you. Now you two get up to house and get cleaned up."
They walked up to the house, and Annie met them out in
the backyard

"I am not going anywhere with two boys that smell
like a pigpen. Strip off all your clothes, and I will hose you
off. There is some lye soap over by the well house."

Annie got them all washed off and sent them in the
house to get dressed for town. About that time Fred had
Dobbin hooked up to the wagon and pulled up to the
backyard.

CHAPTER 9

NEW PLAY CLOTHES FOR TROY AND ROY

They all loaded up and drove up the drive to the main road. Dog jumped in the back of the wagon just as they turned out on the road. After they went up the road a ways, they caught up on Dan running down the road. "Fred, isn't that Clare's horse, Dan?" said Annie.

"Yes," said Fred.

"Are you going to stop and help her put him back up?" Annie asked Fred.

"Yes! I guess so," Fred said. "I should just turn my head and keep on driving by." Annie said, "Now what does that mean?"

"Just wait and you see," Fred said.

When they got to Clare's house, Fred stopped the wagon and Clare came out to the road. Fred said, "Has Dan been opening the gate again?"

"Yes, he will not close a gate behind himself," Clare said.

Fred got down and went back up the road, and Dan came right up to him. Fred stretched out his hand and caught him by the halter, and he led him back up the road to the barn. Annie stood and talked to Clare until Fred got back with Dan. Clare couldn't help noticing how big the boys have gotten since the last time she had seen them. Fred put Dan back in the lot by the barn. Clare thanked Fred for helping catch Dan and putting him back in the lot. Annie bid Clare a good day and said they would see her at church on Sunday.

When they got to town, Fred dropped off some plow points at Joe's blacksmith shop to be sharpened. The boys had never seen so many tools and machines before. Out back he had some young ponies that he was selling. That really got Roy's attention. Fred knew the way Roy looked at those ponies that he had not heard the end of that. But nothing was said about them or anything else. The boys were still taking everything in; there were a lot of new things to see.

Fred said that they would stop by on their way back home to pick them up if they are ready.

They got down to Berkemeyers' dry goods store.

Annie took them in and Mr. Auto met them at the door. Annie introduced the boys.

Annie said, "They are going to be staying with us all summer, and they would need some play clothes."

He had just their size.

It didn't take very long, and he was boxing the new clothes up. And they were on their way back out.

Fred and Dog were still setting in the wagon.

Fred said, "Are we already to go back home."

"I think so," Annie said.

"Do you want to stop at C&D Drugstore and get one of those Coke floats?" Roy and Troy hadn't had one of those before but it sounded good, and they were willing to try anything new. As they were walking up the sidewalk, Troy saw a little kitten coming up the sidewalk and stopped and picked it up.

Annie said, "Put that kitten down. It will give you ringworms." Troy looked at Roy and said, "What are ringworms?"

Fred spoke up and said, "You don't want them, just put it down."

Troy dropped the kitten and the kitten ran away. Then Troy looked at Roy again.

"What's a ringworm?"

John the county agent was walking up the sidewalk to his office and saw the boys with Fred and Annie.

"Hey, are these the little boys that are staying with you all summer?" said John.

Annie spoke right up, "They sure are, there are my favorite grandchildren."

"Well, I can see they sure look like little Kathy when she was young," John said.

Fred said, "They want to learn how to be farmers when they grow up." That was all John needed to here; he was always ready to talk to someone about the life of farming.

He went into his office and brought out coloring books, colors, papers on planting, even a farmer's almanac.

John asked if he could take them out to some farms with him and show them what a county agent job is and how they helped the area farmers.

Fred said, "I will be cutting that acre of sorghum pretty soon, and I think I will teach the boys how to make some sorghum molasses. That will be good for them to know, you know I think that's going be a lost art."

"Not many people still make their own molasses anymore," John said.

"If you can use me I would like to come out and give you an extra hand."

"Sure can, it will be me, Frank, and the boys. Thanks for asking."

CHAPTER 10

LEARNING HOW TO BE A FARMER

Everyone got loaded up and Dobbin headed home. On the way home the boys was coloring in their new coloring books.

Roy asked, "Grandpa, what is sorghum?"

"It is like really heavy syrup made from sorghum cane," Fred said.

"I have an acre down below the barn that will be about ready to cut before you boys will be leaving to go back home. We will have to cut it and let it dry a little and run it though a cane mill. Then we will have to cook it down and that's what makes the molasses," said Fred.

"What do you use it for?" Roy asked.

Mostly feed for our livestock. "And you also cook with it. You can use it like sugar," Fred said.

"After we get all we need, the rest will be taken into town at the co-op, and they will buy it. They use it for making sweet feed for the milk dairies around here. Is that what you feed Bessie??"

"Yes it is," said Annie. "That's what keeps her waiting at the gate at feeding time, and the fact that she is ready to be milked."

This was midafternoon when they got back home. "It's too late to think about doing anything today, so why don't we go down to the White Oak Creek and see if we can catch some catfish for supper tonight.

"How's that sound, Annie?"

"If you can catch some flathead catfish, bring them home. That is the best eating," Annie said.

The boys' face lit up when Fred said fishing; they had never been fishing before. Annie told the boys they better not bring home any mud cats to be cleaned. They didn't know the different between mud cat and flathead cat.

Annie took the boys down by the road where some cane was growing. She helped them cut some cane poles to use to fish with. Fred got the hooks and line from the toolbox.

Fred said, "Annie, do you want to go with us?"

"No, I need to stay here and get some housework done, just go on and have a good time."

The boys had lots of questions about what and how to fish.

Fred said, "Hey wait a minute, the one thing I want to teach you about fishing is, you have to slow down and take it easy. There may not even bite, and if they don't it's a good afternoon to take a nap under this big oak shade tree, lying back on the side of the creek bank. If nothing else, you can take your shoes off and put your bare feet in the cool water. That's really living it up around here."

Fred knew just where to find some big night crawlers for fish bait, right under a big tree next to the creek.

Fred said, "Boys, here all you have to do to find fish bait. Just rake the leaves back with your hands and fill your pockets. No, don't put them in your pockets."

I brought a pail to put them in. It took about five minutes to pick up all the night crawlers for fish bait that they would need. Fred got everyone's lines all fixed up and they started to fish.

Fred said, "The Good Book says, 'Give a man a fish and he will eat for a day. Teach a man to fish, and he will eat for a lifetime.' And he will never go hungry. You boys remember that."

Well, it was all serious for a while, then they sat down on the bank of the White Oak Creek under a big oak tree; it was a warm afternoon and a perfect day for fishing. They were not getting much action on their fishing lines, so they started talking. Fred was telling them all kinds of stories, anything to keep them laughing. And Roy asked Fred, "Why do you like farming so much?"

Fred said, "Because at times like these you got everything planted, everything has come up looking pretty good. We can use a little more rain. But you take whatever you get, can't do anything about old Mother Nature."

"Who's Mother Nature?" said Troy?

She is in control of all nature and weather, said Fred.

Troy looked at Roy and shrugged his shoulders.

Troy asked, "How do you know when the soil is right and it's time for planting?"

Fred said, "In the early spring when you can take the toe of your boot and kick up a clump of fescue grass, well it's time to start breaking ground."

Fred said, "When you get it all turned over, good and loosened up, then get you about a snuff lid full of dirt and throw it in your mouth."

Troy asked, "How much is a snuff lid full?"

Fred said, "About a teaspoon full. If it tastes salty or if it burns your mouth, you may want to put some lime in it before you plant. Hey you're going to be a farmer. Don't be afraid to eat your own dirt off your own ground. And always use you farmer's almanac. Let that be your planting guide. Never plant anything when the sign is in a veiled part of the body. You do your part getting the ground good and loose and you plant. You have to wait and see what kind of year you will have, too much rain, too dry, cool nights, wet days, or not any rain at all. Every year is different. Just because you had a good year or a bad year the year before don't let that stop you from planting. That's why we like to go fishing. We can't do anything about what the weather is going to do. So we may as well lean back under this oak tree and take a nap."

About the time they all leaned back, Fred said, "Hey I am getting a bite. You boys better check your line."

Fred pulled a big flathead catfish out of the water; it must have weighed at least three pounds.

Roy's line took off. "Pull it up," said Fred.

And he had one that was a little smaller then Fred's fish. They were putting their fish in a box that they were using to keep their fish in until they were ready to leave. Troy's line took off across the creek.

"Pull it up," said Fred.

Fred could tell he had a big fish on his line, so he ran over to give him a hand with his fish.

When they pulled it out of the creek his fish was the biggest. "I think we have enough for supper. Let's load up and go home," said Fred.

All the way home the boys were so excited about their afternoon fishing, they never stopped talking about it. When they got back home, Annie and Fred showed them how to clean catfish. Annie sent the boys out to the garden to pick some ripe tomatoes and lettuce for a salad. They even pulled up a few green onions, and Annie made what she called hush puppies. She made little corn bread balls that had onion in them. It was the best they had ever had, they said. "It's called hunting and gathering. You boys see we fixed the whole meal all right here," Annie said.

Now the boys felt like they really did something big and important.

CHAPTER 11

SATURDAY WASH DAY

It was Saturday, and it was wash day for Annie. She was up at 6:00 a.m., ready to get started. She went in to wake up the boys. "Troy, you and Roy get up, breakfast is ready," Annie said.

They heard breakfast and they were ready for that, so they got up came into the kitchen rubbing their eyes. "What time is it?" asked Roy.

"It is 6:00 a.m. Saturday and it is wash day. I don't want this to turn into an all-day job, so eat your pancakes and syrup," Annie said.

Annie didn't have to tell those boys to eat, just put it down in front of them and get back out of the way. About five minutes later, they had eaten all the pancakes she had fixed, and she was making one more for Fred.

When Roy said, "Can I have one more?" Fred looked at Annie with his eyes bugged out.

"Poor Kathy and Jim. I don't know how they will ever feed these boys in a few more years," said Annie.

"They do like your cooking," said Fred.

Annie said she was going out to start a fire under the iron pot, and she would be needing some water in it soon.

"You boys get dressed and come outside in the backyard."

Well, Annie made this wash day sound like a lot of fun last night. The boys had never had a wash day before. They were excited to get their day started. So they hurried up got dressed and went out to the backyard. Annie had already gotten a good fire started under the steel pot.

Annie said, "I need six buckets of water in this pot, six buckets in the rinse tub, and six buckets in the washing machine."

Roy looked at the well pump and had seen three buckets sitting beside it.

Roy said, "Those are big buckets. We will have to double team them."

They had a hand pump to get water out of the well. You had to pour some water down the top of the pump to prime the pump before it would pump water. Roy poured water down the top of the pump, and Troy started pumping. It worked, and soon they were pumping water. They filled all three buckets and then started carrying water to put in the steel pot.

Then they started filling the rinse tub while the steel pot water was getting hot.

By that time Troy said, "My arms are getting longer. Are yours, Roy?"

"No, keep on pumping or we will never get done." And he sat the buckets down by the water pump. They filled all the tubs, machine, and steel pot and then it was time to start to wash the clothes. That was a lot better; it gave our arms time to rest.

Grandma Annie put some clothes in the washing machine and turned it on. It went to sloshing around and started making some bubbles, with the lye soap she put in it. Then she stated putting the clothes though the ringers, and it smashed all the water out of them.

Then she put it in the rinse water.

Then we had to smash the water out of them again.

Then she put them in a basket to be hung out.

That was the easy part.

It also meant we were about done.

Troy liked this part. He was too short to hang up the clothes on the line. So he handed the clothes to Grandma Annie and Roy.

That made everything go a lot faster. It took about the whole morning to do the washing. I just don't know why Grandma Annie was so excited last night about wash day; it was not fun at all. In fact it was a lot of hard work. Troy said, "If she thinks that was fun, we need to tell Grandpa Fred to have a talk with her."

"I think she may be losing her mind a little bit," Roy said.

After all of the clothes was hung up on the line to dry, Annie said, "You boys could go play but don't go far."

She thanked them for helping her, and she would have a big lunch just for them in a little while. The boys went out to see what Grandpa Fred was doing in the back of the barn.

"Did you boys get all your washing done?" Fred asked.

Troy said, "Grandpa, you need to have a talk with Grandma. She acted like that was fun. It was a lot of hard work. I thought my arms were going to fall off carrying all that water."

"Well, ever since I got her that new automatic washing machine, she has been like that on wash day. Just be glad you don't have to go down to the creek and beat the clothes clean on a rock like she used to."

Roy looked at Troy and smiled.

CHAPTER 12

HELPING NEIGHBORS

"Grandpa, what are you working on?"

"I am going to take this old mowing machine to the Joneses. They just moved in down the road in the old Miller place. They are going to be cutting hay on Monday. I got me a new mowing machine last year, and I think they could use my old one. It is still in very good shape. I just wanted a bigger one," said Fred.

"They are going to need our help tying the hay bales and hauling them to the barn."

"I will tell you."

"This won't be a lot of fun."

"But it will be a lot of work."

"But they need our help, and Mr. Jones just has a small boy that is about your age. And he won't be a lot of help. I told Bill that we wanted to help him and Frank," said Fred.

We will need them to help us when we cut our sorghum. That is one thing you need to learn to do if you are going to be farmers, sometimes you have to help one another. Sometimes you get spread thin when things need to be cut or picked or even hauled to the market; you have to jump in and help.

You don't want to see a good man loose crops because of not having help or the time to get all the work done.

Frank is the town handyman; he does work for people all over the valley. When someone needs an extra hand, they call on Frank; he can do about anything.

He has a stationary baler that he will pull out to the hay field, and we will have hand-fed the baler and hand-tied the bales.

"We will need about four men, Frank, Bill, and me. And you three boys will be enough to get it all done," said Fred.

Well, Bill got everything cut down on Monday, and then we had to wait until the grass dried out before we could bale it.

Troy asked, "Why do you have to wait till it dries out before you can bale it?"

Fred said, "If you don't let it dry, the hay has too much moisture in it, and the hay will mold and will make the animals sick if they eat it."

So on Wednesday we went over to get started on Bill's hay. When we got over there, we meet the little boy. He was eleven years old. His name was Michael, and they called him Mickey for short. He was a big kid to just be eleven years old, and that boy was as strong as a bull calf.

He didn't seem very bright, but he worked very hard, and all the boys got along very good. I was very proud of my boys to have been raised in the city and never been on a farm before. They worked very hard. It was lunchtime, and Annie had brought over for us some food to help Catharine with the meal. She knew just how our boys would eat. Sure enough, those two boys made Annie proud; they were eating so fast that everyone else just stopped and watched until they were though, before they started eating again.

Bill looked over at Fred and said, "Did you not feed them breakfast before you come over this morning?"

"Oh yes, they eat like this every meal. Poor Annie. I don't know what she's going to do with them."

After everyone finished eating lunch, they went right back to work on the hay. At about 7:00 p.m. we had all the hay baled and put in the barn. Bill was very grateful for all the help and said he would be over to help with making the sorghum molasses, when it was ready to cut. Mickey and the boys had a lot of fun playing in the hayloft, after they stacked the hay. I just don't know where they get all their energy.

Fred looked at Bill and said, "I wished I just had one-third of their energy. Why don't you let Mickey come over and play with Troy and Roy some? It will be good for them. Mickey is a very good boy, you should be very proud of him."

CHAPTER 13

GOING TO THE LIVESTOCK AUCTION

Bill said they were going to the county line livestock auction on Friday. "You and the boys are welcome to come with us if you like. I have some young calves I need to sell, and I need to buy a new bull," said Bill.

"The boys have never seen a livestock auction before. That will be good for them," said Fred.

"We will be leaving about eleven thirty right after lunch. If you can meet me over here, we all can go together," said Bill. "We will see you at eleven on Friday."

Well, Friday came and the boys were excited about going to see all the cattle.

"Why do farmers take their cows to sell them at the auction?" asked Roy.

Fred said, "They will be cattle buyers there buying up all the young three-hundred- to five-hundred-pound calves and take them to feedlots. That's where they will put more weight on them, and then they take them to the packing house. That's when they go to the supermarkets where people can buy meat for their homes."

Bill had a big truck with sideboards on it where he loaded the six calves in. We all squeezed in the cab of the truck with Grandpa and Bill.

There was plenty of room for all of us. We laughed all the way to the auction. Grandpa was having a good day telling us stories when he was younger. We got there at 1:00 p.m., and the sale started at 1:30. So we had time to check in the cafes and go in the arena and sit and wait on the sale to start. We were about to sit down when a little man came up to us. He had a little pig with him. He had the shiniest head you have ever seen.

Fred said, "Little John, how are you and Missy doing?"

"I brought in a few pigs, and Missy is not very happy about that. She has been squealing ever since I loaded them up. I just hope she doesn't start that when the sale starts." Little John walked away and climbed to the top of the bleachers to sit down,

"Who was that, Grandpa?" Roy asked.

Fred said, "That was Little John and his pet pig, Missy."

"He sure had a shiny head," said Roy.

Bill said, "Him standing under that light, I was thinking I should have worn my sunglasses on. That shiny head was about to blind me."

They started out the sale with some odds and ends. Roy asked Fred, "Why does that auctioneer sound like that? It's like he is trying to sing, but he is not very good."

Fred said, "Well, he has to use expression in his voice so that keeps everyone's attention, so they can follow along with the bid on the item that's being sold. It helps people concentrate on what he is saying."

Troy said, "I still can't understand what he is saying."

"You will after you get used to him," said Fred.

They sat there and watched all kinds of livestock sell for three or four hours. Then they started to sell the bulls. Bill wanted to buy a Hereford bull; they are red and white and usually very gentle. Bill picked him out a real nice young bull. And after that they started selling the pigs, and just as soon as the pigs came into the arena Missy started squealing so loud no one could hear anything that anyone was saying. Finally Little John started down the bleachers with Missy and tripped over her and fell down the last set of steps. Of course he banged his head on the bars that went around the arena, busted his head open again, and everyone started laughing. Finally someone helped him up and got a rope on Missy, so he could drag her out and put her in his truck. It took a while for everything to get settled down.

The auctioneer said, "Let's everyone take a short break. I need to go to the bathroom after all that laughing."

Bill said, "We have got what we came after so what you say we load up and head home?"

CHAPTER 14

WATERMELON PICKING TIME

Bill got the bull loaded up and we started home. Fred and Bill laughed almost all the way home at little John and Missy. Fred said he was spoiling that pig so bad that when Missy gets to be four hundred or five hundred pounds, little John will have his hands full with her. We got back to Bill's house, and Fred thanked them for letting everyone go to the auction with them. Our watermelons are starting to ripe; we have pickers coming in from the city. They are going to take all of our melons to a big wholesale produces company. My first big load will be going to Polly's market.

"If you have some time on Saturday, I would like to hire you to haul a load to town. Old Dobbin will be happy about that. We can't haul as many on the wagon as you can on your truck."

Bill said, "He would be over early on Saturday."

Saturday came, and it didn't take long to load up Bill's truck. Fred always grew Black Diamonds and Charleston Gray; that was the variety most people wanted. The pickers would be there on Monday. So we had all we needed for the Polly's market by noon. Dobbin didn't get out of it altogether. Fred used him and the wagon to drive through the middle of the field; it made picking up the watermelons easier to load. Roy, Mickey, Bill, and Grandpa Fred walked alongside the wagon. Troy got to drive Dobbin. He really thought he was doing a lot. He wasn't strong enough to pick up the big melons. Grandpa Fred made him feel big and important getting to drive Dobbin and the wagon.

Fred said, "Troy, I think you have found your calling. You are doing an excellent job driving old Dobbin."

Fred knew that Dobbin really didn't need anyone to drive him. He had walked up and down melon patches so many times, he could do it blindfolded. They got all the melons loaded up in Bill's big truck, and they started to town. When they got to Polly's market, people were already lining up to buy Fred's watermelons.

Everyone said that Fred could grow the sweetest melons in the county. That made Troy and Roy feel very proud of their Grandpa Fred. They unloaded some on the sidewalk and they took the rest inside."

Fred said, "This has been a long day. Let's go home and help Annie with the feeding and milking."

By the time everyone got back home, Annie almost had everything done. She did save the milking for Fred. While Fred and the boys was finishing up with the feeding, Annie went in and fixed supper. She fixed extra because she knew that those two boys would be very hungry. By the time they got up close to the house, Roy could smell supper cooking and broke out into an all-out hard run and Troy right behind him. I thought those two boys would tear the back door off its hinges getting in the house. They made Annie proud, she didn't have anything left. Most of the time, whatever is left over from last night's supper goes into the pigs' slop so the pigs could have it to eat the next morning. Annie looked at Fred and said, "I guess the pigs won't have anything but shorts and water with their feed in the morning. After that, everyone went in and sat down in the living room and talked about what happened that day. Annie looked over at the boys and they were already asleep.

She said, "Fred put them to bed. You wore them out."

Well, Monday came and the pickers showed up to pick the watermelons. They had four big trucks. After looking at the melons, they said they hoped they brought enough trucks. The man that was in charge said, "Fred, you outdid yourself this year. We would like to give you thirty cents a melon. You and Mrs. Annie keep a count as we bring them to be loaded."

They had a new tractor with a lift on the front of it. They had big boxes that would just hold so many melons. It took them about all day to get all the melons picked. But finally they were done. And it was a welcome sight for Fred and Annie. To see all them go, Annie said, "If we can get rid of our peanuts that easy, it will be a blessing."

Fred said, "Boys, it will be peanut-pulling time in a week or so." Roy looked at Troy and said, "I have seen that peanut patch, and do you think we will have to pull all those peanuts up one by one?" Fred looked at Annie and smiled. He had already had the boys out pulling up weeds so they knew what pulling meant.

CHAPTER 15

HARVEST TIME

Well, the days were long and full of things to do. Everyone was sleeping very well and sound. Troy and Roy were wondering why Fred and Annie always went to bed so early. Now they knew that they went to bed as soon as they have eaten their supper. It was time to harvest the peanuts. Fred called on Frank; he had a harvester that he used to help people in the valley with their peanut crops from time to time.

Fred said he didn't know what people would do around here if it weren't for Frank. He all ways stayed so busy that he hardly had time to get his own things done sometimes. His peanut harvester would dig the peanuts and separate the dirt from the roots and the vines, and all you had left were the peanuts that you had to let dry out for a few weeks, which were then ready to roast and eat. Most of the peanuts would be sold to the local peanuts company. They would send a truck up and haul them to their plant and then would process them into peanut butter and peanut oil. Troy and Roy was very interested in Frank's new peanut harvester; it was fascinating how it worked. Troy looked at

Fred and said, "Grandpa, I sure thought we were going pull all the vines by hand like we do the weeds."

Fred laughed. "Well, boys, this is progress. We used to have to do things like that. Now with new inventions like these, farmers can plant more knowing they have the equipment to do the job in a lot less time. It would take us days to do what we can do now in an afternoon."

Frank had the ten acres of peanuts finished in just a few hours. Planter's peanut truck was sitting waiting for him to dump the harvester. After Frank got to go back up to the barn and was about to home, Annie came out and said, "Frank, you have got stay for supper. I have already fixed you a plate, we are having fried chicken." Well, Frank had already had Annie's fried chicken at the church house for Sunday dinners. She could make the best fried chicken in the county. That was all she had to say, and Frank jumped off the harvester and said, "Where can I wash up?"

About that time Troy and Roy heard what was said, they took off running as fast as they could to the back door of the house.

And Annie right behind them ran as fast as she could. Frank said, "Mrs. Annie can still pick her feet up pretty well for a woman her age. What's her hurry?"

Fred said, "She knows if she don't get in the kitchen behind those two boys by the time we get there there won't be anything left for us to even get a smell of."

She worked hard on a good supper for everyone. In five minutes' time those two boys can have the whole table completely cleaned off.

Annie can't fill those two up no matter what she sets down in front of them. They have the best appetite of anyone I have ever seen. Annie has a full-time job just cooking for them. I am beginning to think that's why Kathy sent them down to stay with us for the summer to give her a break from fixing for them.

Annie kept the boy away from the table until Frank and I came in the back door.

Oh it did smell good.

We all sat down and had a good meal. Everyone got all they could eat, even the boys. Frank got ready to leave. Fred said, "We will be cutting our sorghum next week. Kathy and Jim will be here in two weeks to pick up the boys. I told them that I would show them how to make sorghum molasses before they went back to Chicago. I will sure miss having them around here. They have been so much help to Annie, and I sure hope they will be able to come back next year."

CHAPTER 16

MAKING SORGHUM MOLASSES

It was a little bit early to cut sorghum, but Fred wanted to make sure the boys got in on helping to make the molasses. The sorghum had done real well this year. Those stocks are twelve feet tall. That should make fifty gallons. "Troy, you make sure you take home at least one or two gallons when you leave," Fred said.

"That will hold you over until you boys come back next year, and we will make some more."

That was the first time anything was said to the boys about coming back next year. Roy said, "We sure want to come back and help you and Grandma. There is too much for you two around here to keep up with."

"Thank you, Roy, it makes me feel proud to hear you say that. Your grandma and I sure have enjoyed having you two boys with us this summer. I hope that you have learned something."

"We sure have," said Troy.

"Never bother a sow with baby pigs."

"Never get in a pen with a Jersey bull."

"And Saturday wash day is not as fun as Grandma. Thanks it is, it's hard work."

Frank brought his stationary cane mill over and set it up. After we cut the sorghum down, we brought it up to the cane mill. We had to stack it standing up, so that it would dry out for four days. This would help the sugar come up. When it was time to put it in the cane mill, we had to hand feed all the cane though two rollers that mashed the juices out of the cane. It drained down a trough into a big tub. From there it went into a big vat that had a fire under it. That would boil it off for a while. Then we poured it though some jelly bags; this would strain out any bits and pieces of the stalks that may have fell in the sorghum. Then it went into a big tub and it cooled down. When it was cool enough that you could stand to touch a fruit jar, we started filling the jars and putting lids on, and boxing them up to take into town.

This was a long day. But it was not a hardworking day; we had a lot of help: Bill, Frank, and John, Fred and the three boys. When all of the sorghum was pushed though the cane mill, Troy, Roy, and Mickey were finished for the day. So they went on their way playing. This was a good day for the men to slow down and just tell stories and laugh and have a good time. The three boys came back just in time to start filling jars. It was not long until all the jars, bottles, and buckets were all full. We finished cleaning up everything, and then put all the tools up that we used. Bill, John, and Frank started to leave and when each of them left all they took with them was a quart jar full of molasses.

Roy and Troy was standing by Fred and said, "Grandpa, is that all they get for working all day here for us?"

Fred said, "Yes, they made a grand total of one dollar twenty-five for all their hard work."

"Boys, listen to me. That's why you need to surround yourself with good, caring people. I do the same thing for them sometimes. We look out for each other. If one of us needs help, we jump in and help. Never let a good man lose a crop because he doesn't have enough help to get it in. If you boys grow up and want to live around Cutter's Crossing, you will live in the best town in the whole country."

Troy said, "Grandpa, but they really worked very hard today."

Fred said, "Those are good caring men, and they care about us. They want us to do well. When you boys grow up you will have friends like this, and you find yourself doing the same thing for them. It is something about living here in this town. It gets in your blood and changes a man. You have deep roots that will stand when times get tough you will know what to do."

CHAPTER 17

VISIT FROM CATHY AND JIM

It was the first week of September, and Kathy and Jim were coming to get the boys in one week. Fred said, "What are you going to do when the boys leave and go back home with their mother and father?" Annie said, "I just don't know. They have been such a good help for me. It's not going to be the same around here, that's for sure. The pigs will probably be happy they will be getting a little something in their slop besides shorts and water." Fred laughed. "I want to take them into town so they can tell everyone bye. John wanted to take them around to some farms in the valley so they can see how a county agent helps the farmers."

The next day everyone got everything done up early so they could get to town. On the way to town they stopped by Clare's house. Frank was out helping her pick her apples. They were so many apples that the trees' limbs were breaking off.

Clare said, "You boys get out and get Mrs. Annie a basketful of apples. She may want to make some applesauce for this winter."

Troy looked at Fred and said, "Have you ever seen so many apples before?"

Fred said, "Clare you should have told us what kinds of apple crop you had this year, and we would have been over to help you get them all picked."

Clare said, "These we are picking now are for us and to take to town to the coop. Welch's will have some pickers here on Friday next week to pick the rest. They will be taking them to the city to be made into juice. But if the boys want to try their hand in apple picking, let them come over in the morning. Frank and I are about finished for today."

Fred said, "Annie and the boys will be back in the morning to give you a hand. I will bring Dobbin and the wagon, and we can help you and Dan haul a load into town."

"Thanks," said Clare.

Fred and Annie and the boys went on into town. They went into Polly's market as Annie needed a few things. While they were in the store, Fred had seen some of the men that were in there from time to time.

Little John was in there with his pet pig Missy. He was talking to Polly about a headlight for his coon hunting. He was planning on going coon hunting tonight. Fred asked, "Little John, how is Missy doing with her coon hunting?" "Well," said Little John, "persimmons are ripe now, and if there is one thing that likes persimmons more than a raccoon, well that would Missy. It seems like every persimmon tree we come up to will have at least three or four coons in it. But Missy would not pay any attention to the coons for all the persimmons. She ate her fill last night and so did I."

"Well, good luck with coon hunting," said Fred. Fred walked away

Troy said, "Grandpa, is that the man we saw at the livestock auction?"

"Yes, he likes to go coon hunting at night," Fred said. "He keeps the fur and sells it down at the coop on Saturdays. There's a man that will buy all the hides you can bring in to him."

Roy said, "That pig is a little strange, Grandpa."

"Now, Roy, leave him alone. He's a pig farmer. That's how he makes his living, and he does very well at it."

Polly came over and spoke to Fred and the boys.

He reached down and pinched Troy on the arm and said, "Looks like Mrs. Annie may have put some weight on this boy and looks like you put some muscle on him too." Fred looked at Troy and said, "Now, Polly, don't say that about anyone unless it's so." Troy looked over at Roy and smiled. He felt a lot bigger like he had ready done something.

John the county agent was in Polly's store and asked Fred if he could take the boys out to the Smith's farm. Fred said, "That would be great."

They live out at east of town. They grow corn and have a big cattle ranch and also milk dairy.

John picked the boys up about nine thirty the next morning. He was driving a truck that the state lets him drive when he is doing agent work.

They got there and Mrs. Smith was expecting the boys, and had a special tour ready for them.

John had to go out and take some samples from his corn plants.

Mrs. Smith showed the boys around the feedlot where they feed out the young calves out for the market. They went into the milk dairy were they had all of their automatic milking machines. The boys were amazed on how the cows were milked, and all the milk went into a huge tank to be picked up every day.

John had the samples from the corn he needed and had to take them back to his office to test them.

He told Mr. Smith that he would take the boys back to the office and they could help him finish the test on the samples.

The boys thanked Mr. Smith for showing their farm to them.

Mr. Smith asked them if they would like to have a farm like this when they get older.

Roy spoke right up. "I sure would. It looks like a lot of work."

"It sure is. You have to get up early and work late sometimes. But not every day. The cows have to be milked and fed every day. We love this life caring for all of our animals. There is a new invention coming up all the time that makes it easier for the farmers to make a profit. And having good people like John here to help you through any problem you come up against, it makes a farmer's life a lot better."

They got back home midafternoon and were very excited to tell Annie and Fred what all John had showed them at the Smith ranch.

Troy said he wanted to be a county agent when he grows up. "Grandpa, John has a very important job. And the farmers need him to help them with their farming problems. Fred said, "Troy, you stay in school and do good.

You have to have a good education to be an agent." Roy said he wanted to have a big ranch like that when he grows up. Fred looked at Annie and smiled. The next day Jim and Kathy came after the boys. Annie and Fred were so glad to see them. The boys were not ready to go back home, but it was good to see their mom and dad. They had so much to tell them. The first thing that Jim noticed was how much the boys had grown over the summer.

Annie said that everyone all over the valley were so proud of the boys and that the boys were so much help that everyone was happy to make the boys' stay so joyful for them. They have so much to take back to school with them that they have learned this summer.

Fred said, "These two boys have done a lot of growing this summer. I am very proud of them, and when you have heard what all they have learned, you will be too. I hope next summer they can come back, and we can see if they remember what they learned this year."

CUTTER'S CROSSING

Story Two

Clare Bell's Famous Home

Made Cheese or Is It?

CONTENTS

INTRODUCTION

This story is during the 1950s. It was a small town right in the middle of some of the best farmland in the South. People had to count on each other, family and neighbors, to help them do their farming that was done the hard way. It took a lot of hands so big families were very common in these days. Land ownership were few. Most people in these days were sharecroppers, which meant they worked for a part of the crops, so they helped do all the farming. Then at harvest time they could sell their part. Some years were better than others.

Mrs. Clare Bell was a widowed lady, very strong willed. Her children had grown up and left home. All of her neighbors helped out whenever they could. Her young son married a little girl named Bettie Joe who worked down at the coop with her mother and father. Her mother never taught her how to cook. As soon as they finished school, they were off to the city. Willard had a job working at the tractor company from up north. He helped design and build tractors. Clare Bell's old milk cow was giving so much milk, she wanted to make some cheese to make better use of the milk. That there was not so much wasted. After she asked around for a cheese recipe, there was not any shortage of help from her neighbors. Isn't it something how you can always find plenty of people that have the best recipe for making whatever it is you are making at the time? Read and see how this works out for Clare and her family.

CHAPTER 1

❦

KNOW YOUR FARMER, KNOW YOUR FOOD

Delbert's Story Time

3-10-13

Once upon a time there lived a lady near a small town called Cutter's Crossing. It was in the heart of some of the best farmland in Flat Rock County. I never knew why they called it Flat Rock because there were no rocks for miles around. This was all sandy-bottomed land. It was great for growing corn, cotton, peanuts soybeans, and about any kind of vegetable or fruit you could think of or wanted to grow.

Clare had lived on this farm her whole life. Clare's mother and father came from Germany and moved down here from up north and settled on the land. There was nothing here but a store at a crossroad.

The railroad came through this part of the state, and this crossroad became very vital for the part of the state. The land was easy to clear and easy to farm. This brought more settlers to the valley, and not long after, a town was started.

This story begins in the 1950s, and it had been more than seventy years since Cutter's Crossing become a town. It was hard times for everyone as there was a drought in the thirties that they called the dust bowl. It was so bad that no one could grow anything. People's water wells were running dry, and there was no water for anyone. Some people had to move away from their farms.

We were some of the lucky ones. Our ponds dried up, and there was not any water for the livestock to drink, so we had to water them out of our water well. Just as it looked like we were just about out of water in our water well, they started trucking water to all of us who were left in the valley from up at the big city. The governor of our great state will never know how much the people around Cutter's Crossing were so thankful for what he did for everyone. The whole summer it was so hot and dry that we couldn't grow anything. We managed to finally get some turnips to grow late in summer. That was all we and our livestock ate all winter. I never ate turnips cooked so many ways, but we were very thankful for what we had. It was a very humbling time for everyone.

We all had to help put our efforts together so we could all make it through the hard times. After that it was like it just stuck with all the people around here. You know when hard times come, and it will, you help one another. If not for all the caring and loving people in our town, I don't know what we would have done. The people around here in Cutter's Crossing are still like that today. It was a good lesson for everyone. When you put your faith and trust in the one that cares the most about you, even though times get tough, you and your family will make it through.

Then our nation was at war in the forties. We lost a lot of good young men from the valley during this time. We had good, caring families here, and they wanted to protect our great country. So when the nation called on our young men, they were ready to be the first to sign up for service.

Clare never could understand why a man would leave a wife and three teenage children and a farm to fight in a war in some faraway land. He told Clare that he felt that he wanted to do his part in protecting his family from anything that could harm them.

The day Willard Bell left, Clare never thought that it might be the last time she would ever see him alive. They said he was a hero and Clare got a metal and a piece of paper signed by the President of the United States thanking him for his brave actions in combat. They said because of him a lot of men lived to tell of his bravery that day. It looked like there would be no way to get though the heavy fighting in combat, but because of Willard Bell's action and quick thinking, the whole platoon was led into safety that day. Clare and her three children were very proud of Willard. He was a good friend, father, and husband and would be missed very much by all.

Clare was known for her sweet potatoes and apples that she grew every year. Everyone looked forward to being the first to buy those as soon as they got ripe.

Clare's father had planted an apple orchard more than forty years ago. Clare said, "Those apple trees just get better every year." She had red and golden delicious, Gala and Granny Smith apples. The Granny Smith apple is what she would use for her applesauce that she would put up for the winter. The Granny Smith apple would also keep as much as six months in her root cellar or a cool dry place.

Everyone all over the valley were farmers in those days. That was the way they made their living. No one had anything much in those days, so there was not much of anything to buy.

People never forgot, for a long time after the war it seemed like there were shortages on about everything you could think of like metal, cloth, leather, and even copper. They stopped making pennies out of copper and started making them out of metal so bullets could be made from copper. Then soldiers on the front lines would have ammunition. They were sending everything to the war. Every person in America was affected in some way and did what they could to help out in the efforts to win and end the war. Everyone wanted to see it over as quickly as possible.

A big family was a must as extra hands were needed at picking time. This was also a time when neighbors helped others. If you had something, and someone else needed it, all you had to do was ask and they were glad to help out. They knew if help was needed the favor would be returned to them. Everyone needed a helping hand from time to time.

The days were long and the work was hard, but everyone loved living in the small town called Cutter's Crossing, which was just like one big family. After all the work was done on Saturday afternoon it was slow down time. No one did anything on Sundays. Any work left undone on Saturday afternoon would have to wait until Monday to be finished up. Sunday was a day everyone would go to church and then enjoy a big lunch. All the ladies would bring their favorite dish to eat. After everyone had eaten their fill, sometimes the men would get up a baseball game to pass the rest of the afternoon. That was the thing about Cutter's Crossing. If you knew your farmer, you would know your food.

CHAPTER 2

CLARE'S COUSIN BERNIE

Agriculture had started growing and getting a lot better for all the farmers in the area. The farmers were starting to make money for all of their hard work.

People around the valley started to buy tractors and implements to take the place of their horse-drawn equipment. The farmers could now do more in a half a day with the new tractors than they could do with a team of horses or mules in two days. This let the farmers plant more and become even more profitable. Some of the older generation were the first ones to buy the new equipment. They were amazed how much more they could do with a lot less back-breaking work in a day's time. It just made perfect sense. Why would a man break his back when he could do things so much easier? One thing about getting older was, you would think most of the time a man should get smarter.

This was called progress in those days. The 1950s was a great time for agriculture. New inventions were coming out all of the time. A lot of the older farmers had saved money over the years while years were good, and now they were ready to start spending some of it. They knew this would make their work easer.

Clare had a cousin named Bernice who lived in Wisconsin with her husband, Barney. Bernice was one of the last ones in her class to have a boyfriend, and that happened after she graduated. There was a boy named Barney that Bernice knew from school. He was not very much to look at. He was tall and slim. If he turned sideways, he would look like a pole standing there. But Bernice's dad was Joe Bell. He was Clare's father's brother, which would make Joe Clare's uncle. Well, Uncle Joe was not about to let Barney get away no matter what he looked like.

Barney's mother and father liked to sit at the front of the church, on the left side on Sunday morning. But that was until Barney got old enough to start coming. The little thing was so gassy you could hear him three pews away. The pastor asked them if they could move to the back row so they would not interrupt the church service any more. There was never a more proud mother then Barney's mom. He was just perfect in her eyes.

The poor boy's teeth fell out by the time he was sixteen years old. The boy's mom took him to the city to buy him false teeth. She did not want him to have a complex. Even though he looked a lot different than the other boys, Barney's mom thought the false teeth would give him more confidence. She thought he was a very handsome young man, now even more with his new false teeth. The teeth, they didn't fit very well. Barney had a breathing problem, and he had a touch of asthma. So with every step he took, it sounded like hoots and clicks coming out of his mouth as he was walking. Even when he was sitting down in a chair he would be spinning his uppers or lowers around in his mouth, with all that extra room he had in his mouth, and if he wasn't doing that, he would suck or chomp his teeth. That just drove Bernice's father, Joe, nuts. But he was determined not to let Barney get away. Bernice was really struck on him like honey on a bee. And Bernice could do nothing wrong in Joe Bell's eyes. What Bernice wanted, if Joe had anything to do with it, Bernice would get.

Joe told Kate, Bernice's mother, "We need to do what we can to help that along, or else we may have Bernice living here the rest of her life. I am going hunting. I saw a swamp rabbit down below the barn. You ask her if she can invite him over for some rabbit stew." Who knows, Bernice may even be able to fatten him up and then he may just grow into those teeth.

And that is just what happened. Bernice was a very good cook just like her mother, so she invited Barney over for a good supper. It seemed like everything went wrong. Bernice was so nervous and excited about cooking for Barney that she left the heat turned up a little too long under the rabbit stew, and it was scorched and tasted really bad, but her corn bread came out perfect. Bernice never bothered to taste test the stew as about that time Barney came up to the front door. It didn't matter now it was what it was. Bernice put it down on the table, as Barney came in the front door. Joe and Kate went out the back door to the barn. They went to do all the feeding and wanted them to have a few moments alone. "What's that smell?"

"It sure smells good," Barney said.

It was amazing how good of an appetite Barney had and still stayed so slim.

His mother said everything he eats must just turn into air. He was a gassy thing even from a young kid; she could not get any weight on him no matter how much she fed him. When he was just a baby we would take him to church. We always liked to sit on the second row on the left side up close to the front. But Barney was so gassy you could hear him four pews away. It sounded like a grown man passing gas, so we had to move to the back of the church.

"Well, let's sit down and try it out," Bernice said. She set down a big bowl in front of Barney. His eyes bugged out as big as half dollars.

He took a big taste and liked to have swallowed his false teeth. "Oh my," Barney said. "Pretty good hum," Bernice said.

"Well, it is missing something," said Barney.

He had a puzzled look on his face but wasn't about to say it tasted bad. Bernice picked up a big spoon and took a taste. She spit it out all over Barney's clean shirt.

"Well, I scorched it," Bernice said.

So they had a big laugh after all that. Barney said, "Well, I think from now on we should call you Bernie."

They had sweet milk and corn bread for their supper after all that. He said the sweet milk and corn bread were the best he had ever tasted.

From that day on, Bernice's named was changed to Bernie. She did finally fatten him up as time went on and years passed by.

Clare didn't hear much from them after they moved up to Wisconsin. Barney had a grandpa up there who had a dairy farm. He retired and wanted Barney to take over the farm, so they moved up there to help out.

CHAPTER 3

THREE STRIKES, YOU'RE OUT

Clare had a jersey milk cow named Beverly. She was getting so much milk from Beverly that she didn't know what she was going to do with it. Mostly she was feeding it to the pigs. Then one day she came across some recipes for making cheese that her cousin Bernie had sent her, and she got to thinking that she could make cheese with all that extra milk. It would keep very well and it tasted pretty good with crackers.

The recipe called for rennet. It is extracted from the fourth stomach of a young cow. It contains a number of enzymes that is designed to help these animals digest their mother's milk, and when added to milk, it will cause the milk to coagulate, forming the curds and whey that are so essential in the cheese-making process.

Clare was trying very hard to learn how to make this cheese. The recipe made everything sound very easy. Clare said, "Those people up in Wisconsin really know what they are doing. I need to go to town see if Polly has any idea. I need a big stainless-steel pot to cook off the milk."

Clare went out to get Dan hooked up to the wagon. Dan was a big Belgian plow horse. Clare had Dan since he was one year old. He was the most help to her around the farm. He helped her with all her gardening and took her everywhere she went since she never learned to drive a car. That was one thing that Willard never got around to teaching her before going to the war.

Dan was out below the barn in a big patch of green clover where he liked to spend a lot of his time. There was only one thing he liked better than eating clover and that was lying down next to it, so when he woke up from his nap, he would get up and eat his fill all over again. Dan turned twenty-six years old this fall. He doesn't get around like he used to do, unless you hold up a big pan of buttermilk biscuits. He could still kick up his heels like a three-year colt, when he would get a look at those big fluffy golden-brown biscuits.

Clare was known all over the valley for her buttermilk biscuits. Anyone that had the pleasure of eating them would be talking about them for days.

"Dan, let's go to town to see Polly," Clare said. Dan was always ready to go to town. Polly had a grocery store in town that was one of the oldest stores in Cutter's Crossing. He had about anything a person could possibly want, from food, fruit, canned goods, hardware, plumbing supplies, and even garden seeds. Everyone could do all their shopping and pick up their supplies there. If Polly didn't have it, he could order whatever you needed from one of those Sears and Roebuck catalogs.

Clare saw that Dan had just eaten all the clover he could hold. Now he was lying down for a long nap in the nice soft grass. After eating all that clover, pulling the wagon to town should make him pretty musical, Clare thought to herself. Clare got him all hooked up to the wagon. "Now get up, you old gas bag," said Clare. On the way to town they met Frank coming up the road on his new tractor. Dan didn't know what to think, seeing Frank sitting on it. "Oh my, Frank, that sure is a pretty red tractor," Clare said.

"This red tractor came here from up north. This right here is progress. All the farmers will be getting them one of these pretty soon," Frank said.

Frank was the town handyman and could fix anything. If you gave him a piece of wire, tape, and screwdriver, he could do about anything. He worked for people all over the valley when they needed an extra pair of hands. If someone asked him for help, it didn't matter if he had too much to do at his own house. He would always find a way to get his stuff done and help his neighbor too. "I am proud for you, Frank. As hard as you work, you deserve that new tractor. Oh, by the way, I will need you to cut and bale my alfalfa hay as soon as you can get to it," Clare said.

"I am going to Polly's to get a new stainless-steel pot to cook off some milk. I am going to try my hand in making cheese," Clare said. "Well, good luck. I am going over to Bill Jones's house to disk up his pumpkin patch. You have a good afternoon," Frank said.

Clare got to Polly's market and went inside and asked him for some tips on cheese making. Polly said, "I have a brother that lives up north and he is a cheese maker. I will give him a call and see if he will help out."

Polly got back with his brother, and he told her it was real important that you don't cook it too long or get the heat up to high. He said he would send some rennet tablets that he uses. Clare said, "I think I will try Steve over at the packing house first. I want to make it the real old-fashioned way."

When Clare got over to Steve's packing house, she told him what she wanted to try to make some cheese. Steve spoke up, "Why, I never heard of anyone making cheese around here. What are you going to do with it?"

"I'm going to eat it, Steve," said Clare. "It may be a good way to get good use out of Beverly's milk, so I am not wasting so much of it."

"I wish I could give you a recipe. I sure would like to try some of that cheese. I will ask my wife tonight at home if she knows anyone that may help you figure this out."

On the way back home with her new stainless-steel pot from Polly's market, she met John, the local county agent.

John was a young man in his late thirties, and he helped all the farmers with their farming problems. I just don't know what people would have done without John. He stopped on the edge of the road and rolled down his window. He was driving in his new truck that the state lets him drive. "Where are you headed?" said Clare. "I'm going over to Bill Jones's house to pick some corn samples from him to test them for corn smut and teosinte fungus and other diseases."

"You mean ear rot?" Clare said.

"That's a better name for it because that's what it does," John said. "I have to get back home to see if I can look over the recipe Aunt Bernie gave me on how to make cheese."

"Hey, Clare. I have a recipe at home my mother used. I will bring it to you tomorrow," said John.

"Thanks," said Clare. "Beverly is giving so much milk I have been just feeding the extra to the pigs. I need to make better use of the milk."

"This is an easy recipe, and I think you will like it. I'd best be on my way," John said. "Have a good afternoon."

John drove on down the road. Clare thought, John works so hard for all the farmers around here, day and night if they need him to. We are lucky to have him in the valley with us. Well, now I have three recipes to try out.

"I have always heard three strikes and you're out," Bettie Joe said.

Clare and Dan got back home, and Clare unhooked Dan and turned him into the lot. Dan went back over and started eating the clover he had left. Clare went into the house and started looking over the recipes, trying to decide which cheese she would make first. About that time the party line started to ring; three shorts and a long ring that was Clare's ring tone. She answered the phone, and it was Frank on the other end. "Clare, this is Frank. I looked for my mother's recipe for cheese and I found it."

He said, "Take five gallons of fresh cow's milk, and it will make six pounds of cheese. Then you put in two and a quarter pounds of rennet then bring all that to a boil fifteen minutes. Then take it off the stove. Throw a towel over it and let it cool down till it's at room temperature. Then you spoon it out with a big wooden spoon into a big bean pot lined with wax paper. Cover it with a cotton cloth and then place it in a refrigerator for three days. After that take it out, dump it on a big plate, and serve with crackers."

Clare said, "That sounds real easy."

"Do you remember eating any of it?"

"And what did it taste like?"

"Well, it's been so long and I have eaten so many times, I don't remember. I think, though, it tasted pretty well. I can't be sure," Frank said.

"I will give it a try and I will bring you some over and you can be the first to try it out," said Clare. Clare thought, I will need some wax paper. That means another trip to Polly's market.

It was getting late in the afternoon by this time, so Clare decided to wait until tomorrow to go back to town. Clare had plenty of work to do around the farm. She went out and started pruning some of her apple trees and made a pretty big brush pile in no time at all. Clare thought she would stop for the day and get all of her animals fed. Then she went in the house to make supper. She had some mail from her son Willard Jr. and Bettie Jo, but she liked to wait till suppertime to open her mail if it was from one of her kids. She missed them so very much. She knew if she opened it in the middle of the day she would not be able to get any work done for missing them so much.

After supper she sat down in her favorite chair by the window and opened her letter. It was very good news. Little Willard and Betty Joe were coming for a visit in two weeks. Oh good. Bettie Joe can help me with cheese recipe.

The tractor company from up north wants Willard to demonstrate some new equipment in the valley that he helped design. So all the farmers around can see some of their new equipment. It was just off the assembly line. They want them to be tested out before they put them up for sale. They would be staying for three weeks. It had been a few months since Clare had seen them. It will be so good to see them and spend time with Bettie Joe.

CHAPTER 4

BIG-TIME FARMING
DEMONSTRATION

As the next two weeks passed, Clare told everyone about Willard and Bettie Joe's visit. The day came, and Willard and Bettie Joe drove up the driveway to Clare's house. It was late afternoon, so Clare started to make a good supper for them to welcome them back home. They sat down at the table and started to eat, and you have never heard such *hmm, hmm*. And rolling her eye, Clare asked, "Bettie Joe, is everything, OK?"

Bettie Joe said, "Oh! Everything is so good. I have really missed eating food like this."

Clare looked over at Willard, and he never even looked up or made a sound. He knew, as everyone in Cutter's Crossing knew, that Clare was the best cook in the whole valley or maybe in the whole county. *I think he was really missing my cooking too*, Clare thought.

Clare looked at Bettie Joe and asked her, "What have you kids been eating?"

"Oh, Willard says I am getting better at cooking every day. I tried to buy hamburger meat and smash it out for hamburger steak, but it just turns black and smells up the house, so I have been having a lot of trouble cooking meat," Bettie Joe said.

"I found some canned meat in the grocery store that is called Spam made by Armor Foods. You can open it, dump it on a plate, wrap it with aluminum foil, and it will keep for days in the refrigerator."

Clare looked at Willard, and he rolled his eyes and smiled. "I also found some Armor potted meat that is great with original premium saltine crackers," Bettie Joe added. Clare said, "Potted what?" Then Clare just shook her head and looked over at Willard who was still smiling.

Willard told Clare he had sent all the farmers in the area and most of the farmers all over the whole state an invitation to the farm-equipment demonstration. This was a big thing around the valley, and people were coming in from all over the state. Clare was very proud of Willard Jr. for bringing all the new tractors with all types of equipment to our area. He said, "It was his way of giving back to his community. All the people around Cutter's Crossing are real proud of what Willard has done to bring all this equipment demonstration here for all the farmers in the valley." His tractor company from up north just last year had rolled their one-millionth tractor off their production line. The land around Cutter's Crossing was rich and sandy soil. It finishes out really nice and made the implements and attachment work look real good. This was perfect conditions for trying out the new equipment that Willard and his company had just designed and taken off the production line. They were looking forward to see what their new equipment would do in this good, rich, sandy-bottomed soil.

Everyone was impressed with the new types of equipment. Agriculture was beginning to be a big business in the valley. The farmers were planning to clear more land to expand their fields.

CHAPTER 5

CLARE'S COOKING LESSONS

While Willard was out showing off all the equipment he had brought with him, it gave Clare and Bettie Joe time to bond.

Clare asked Bettie Joe if she had a cheese recipe. "No," said Bettie Joe.

"I don't ever remember ever tasting homemade cheese, just what you could buy from the store. We may as well try the recipe that Frank gave us," Clare said.

Bettie Joe was a young, very pretty and kind girl from the valley. Bettie Joe and Willard had been married for six years. They still did not have any children. Bettie Joe's mother and father ran the co-op downtown. Bettie Joe ran the cash register. If there was one thing Bettie Joe learned from working at the co-op all those years, it was to count. She had to be the smartest person in the whole county when it came to counting. All that time doing inventory counting all those nuts, bolts, screws, and nails really paid off for Bettie Joe.

I always wondered why Willard never passed up a trip to the co-op for feed. When we would go pick some up food for our livestock, I noticed him looking at Bettie Joe, and she was always looking at him, but nothing was ever said between them. She sure was a pretty little thing and very smart. Her mother was so busy at the coop, she never had time to teach Bettie Joe how to cook. Poor girl could not even boil water. But at least she could count better than anyone in Cutter's Crossing. She could always have that to fall back on if she needed to.

Clare asked Bettie Joe while they were here for a visit over the next three weeks if she could give her some cooking tips. First thing Clare asked Bettie Joe was, "What about water?"

"When you boil water you have to wait until the water bubbles before taking it off the stove. Otherwise it's just hot water."

Clare asked Bettie Joe, "Do you have a mixer?"

"No," Bettie Joe said.

"Do you have cake pan or cookie sheet?"

"No."

"Do you have pots and pans?"

"Well," said Bettie Joe. "What do you have?

Clare interrupted. "I have one cast iron skillet and one big soup pot, and one little saucepan," Bettie Joe replied. "What kinds of food do you like to fix?" Clare asked?

Bettie Joe said, "I make a Spam soup that Willard really likes."

Clare looked puzzled. "How do you make that?"

"I take one pound of Armor Spam and cut it in little squares that would easily fit in a spoon, then put it in my soup pan with water until its gets hot," Bettie Joe replied.

Clare batted her eyes. "What else do you make?"

Armor has a potted meat in a can that's really good with crackers. You just spread it on them, and it makes an easy meal when you don't have time to make soup. "OK, what is potted meat?" Clare replied.

"Well, it's kind of like smashed-up Spam in a smaller can, but it tastes really good," Bettie Joe replied.

"A neighbor that lives in the apartment across from us told me about a gravy recipe. Sometimes I pick up a can of Eat Well Bonita Jack mackerel. Then I put it in my small pan with a little flour and fresh milk, turn on the stove till it starts to get thick, then turn it off and serve it with light bread. It makes a great meal," Bettie Joe proudly said. Clare had to turn around to keep a straight face. Clare almost broke down into tears to think her boy had to eat fish gravy.

"Oh, and my neighbor also has a crackling corn bread recipe I want to try. She said it is very good," Bettie Joe said.

Clare said, "Crackling what? You don't eat crackling in cornbread." By this time Clare had heard about all she could stand. Clare was so glad for this visit. This poor girl needed Clare and her cooking tips in the worst way.

Clare turned around and grabbed Bettie Joe and gave her a big hug. And said, "Don't worry, you will be cooking like one of those fancy New York restaurant chefs when you are ready to go back home." Clare knew that she had her work cut out for her, but Bettie Joe was a very smart little girl; she should pick up on this cooking real easy. Clare said, "We have to go down to Polly's grocery store before you go back, so you can pick up some measuring cups and spoons and a new set of pots and pans."

Clare got out a recipe on her buttermilk biscuits. They started looking it over. "How about this one? I will show you how to make sausage gravy to go along with it," Clare said.

Clare thought, This just may be easy. Sounds like she already has the gravy making down. The recipe called for two cups of sifted flour. Then add 3 teaspoons baking powder and one teaspoon salt. Cut in one-fourth cup of shortening until pea-size crumbs form. Add one-fourth cup of buttermilk depending on humidity. Dough will be sticky. Turn out on floured surface and knead in flour until dough pulls away from your hands. Flour a rolling pin and roll dough to one-half-inch thickness. Cut with biscuit cutter and put in cake pan or skillet. Then bake at four hundred degrees for eight to ten minutes.

"That sounds real easy," Bettie Joe said.

"Well, let's try it," Clare adds.

Clare got out all the ingredients that they would need and watched as Bettie Joe started putting them all together, following the recipe closely, then into the oven for ten minutes. Later out they came. They were the prettiest golden-brown biscuits you have ever seen, just picture perfect. Clare said, "Well, what do you think?" Bettie Joe was so surprised with herself. The only things she could say was "Bring on the gravy."

Bettie Joe could not wait until Willard got home so he could try her buttermilk biscuits and sausage gravy. Clare was very proud of her, but she had a lot more she wanted to teach her before the week was out.

As the week went on, the cooking got a lot easier. Bettie Joe was a fast learner, trying really hard to learn all she could and seemed to have a knack for cooking. In no time at all she was cooking pretty well. Clare asked Willard

Jr., "What have you been eating all this time, and why would you eat it?"

"Well, Bettie looked so cute and was trying so hard to make a good supper for me every night. I couldn't tell her that I didn't like it, so I would just hold my breath and swallow it down. Besides it was better than nothing at all. I remember that summer when it was so hot and dry that we could not make a crop. We finally made some turnips that fall. And we had to live on turnips all winter. I told myself that I didn't want to see another turnip the rest of my life. So if there was something to eat besides turnips, I could make myself eat it."

"You poor boy," Clare said. "I am going to work on that while you're here with the tractors. Tomorrow you come home early. I think Bettie Joe will have a surprise for you."

The next day Willard came in about 5:00 p.m. Bettie Joe met him at the front door. "Why don't you go out and help your mother with the feeding? I will have supper ready in one hour," Bettie Joe said.

Willard went out to the barn to help Clare. "It sure is good to come back home, Mom. I sure do miss this place and everyone around here. I wish I could move back here and stay forever. Thank you so much for teaching Bettie Joe how to cook. I was getting pretty tired of the Spam soup and fish gravy." That's when Willard and Clare had a big laugh together.

I ran into little John and his pet pig Missy today. "Don't you think that is a little bit strange?" Willard said. "I think that is a lot strange."

"Well, it's just not normal for a pig to run after coon dogs like that," Clare said. "He said she was very good at treeing coons. He invited me to go on a coon hunt with him before I have to go back home. I think I will. I would like to see this Missy in action."

"I sure miss going hunting with Dad," Willard said. "I think about that a lot."

"Well, you should go. It will be good for you and Little John to spend some time together," Clare said.

About that time, Bettie Joe called them in for supper. By the time they got to the back door of the house, Willard could smell what he thought was fried chicken. Willard looked at Clare and said, "Is that what I think it is?" Willard said, "Mom, you may have to help me to the table. This smells so good I don't know if I make it. Willard and Clare went in, cleaned up, and sat down at the kitchen table. Bettie Joe had fixed fried chicken, mashed potatoes, milk gravy, and corn on the cob, cornbread and sweet tea. She was so proud; she made everything without any help from Clare at all. Willard looked at Bettie Joe and thanked her and gave the blessing for the meal she had prepared and then looked at Clare, and said, "Thanks, Mom."

CHAPTER 6

LITTLE JOHN'S PET PIG MISSY

There was one thing men liked to do when all the work was done, and that was coon hunting. Something about getting out in the night air away from the town streetlights. There is one thing that makes a person feel small. On a clear night you could see every star in the sky. The sound of a whippoorwill calling right as the sun goes down while you are sitting out on your front porch. That is how some people would relax. If you were lucky there was the sound of a hoot owl calling in the middle of the night. Or the sounds of tree locusts and crickets, and the sound of some bullfrogs in a nearby stock pond.

Or maybe the sound of wind blowing through a big pine tree or just the sounds of a crackling campfire. No matter what kind of a day you may have at work, you could put away all the pressures that day had brought you. In just a few minutes after hearing those old coon dogs pick up a trail and take off after a coon, nothing else seems to matter but catching that coon.

Those still dark nights, it seemed like you could hear those old coon dogs barking for a mile away.

Little John was a pig farmer that lived out east of town. He was very good at raising pigs. He had done this for his whole life. His father was a pig farmer before him, so he knew about everything there was to know about raising pigs.

He had been friends with the family for a long time. He was my dad's best friend; they went through school together. Little John and Dad used to go hunting a lot together whenever they got a chance. I would go with them when I was young. I remember going coon hunting at night and sat and make a big campfire and listen to the old coon dogs run after coons. Mostly we would just sit down and listen to Little John tell stories. He had a wild imagination; he was known for stretching the truth little… sometimes a lot. I will never forget sitting watching Dad listen to an old lie he would be telling and laughing till his sides would be hurting.

Little John was a short, round man. He was as strong as a young bull for his age, really light on his feet, and carried himself like a young man. He would be pushing sixty years old by now. If he kept this pace of living up, he would probably be one of those that live to be one hundred years old. He was a good and caring person. A good friend to all of us and anyone else who needed him. He was always there to help us in any way he could. He hardly had any hair on his head. He was completely bald. He had just a small patch of hair around his ears and a little bit on the back of his head. He never wore a hat because with the slightest breeze it would blow off his head. He always had a cut or a bruise on his head from banging his head on something while working in his hog house.

Working for that tractor company up north in the office is making me soft. I just hope I can still keep up with him and his dogs. Even though I am half his age, this will be a good work out for me.

Little John came by and picked me up about 7:00 p.m. as the sun was about to set and it was to just starting to get dark. "Where are we going?" Willard asked.

"Let's get down to the bottoms. I've been having pretty good luck there. There may be more coons north of town but a lot more persimmon trees and the persimmons are ripe now, and there are not as many persimmon trees down here in the bottoms."

"If Missy gets a whiff of those she will quit on us," little John said. "There is only one thing that loves persimmons more than an old coon, and that would be Missy."

Little John turned out his dogs and Missy. The dogs took off barking, and that pig took off grunting every step. "That's amazing," said Willard. Little John got out a metal hard hat with a carbide lamp on it, and he put it on his head and handed a lantern to Willard. Willard asked, "How did you get that big scar on your forehead?"

"Well it's a long story."

Little John started telling what had happened. "Polly's cousin Ralph from Kentucky sells supplies to the coal miners, and I got my new headlight there. They wear them down in those deep dark caves. Polly, not knowing much about them, sold me one without a hard hat so I strapped it on to an old straw hat that I had hanging in my barn. That night when I was coon hunting, I turned on the light and it caught my hat on fire. Oh these things burn really hot, so you best be careful with them. The good thing is, you can see for miles, with these lights on," said Little John.

It was not long when the coon dogs picked up a trail. About that time Missy started squealing, it was so loud in the dark deep woods. You could have heard it for miles around. Then Little John started hollering SOOWEE! SOOWEE! The more he hollered the louder Missy got. We ran down to a big oak tree that had three big coons up almost at the top. Little John said, "You want to have some fun?" There was a big bore coon on a big limb just left of the other ones. "Let's throw some rocks at him see if we can get him to jump out," Little John said.

For an old middle-aged man, Little John can still throw pretty straight and hard. About the second time he threw, he hit the old coon, and he jumped out and the fight was on. Fighting the dogs was no trouble for the coon. The old coon put the dogs on the run pretty quickly, but fighting a pig was a little different. It didn't seem normal to the coon. I think he was a little confused. That old coon ran off over the hill.

We picked up the other two coons, and the dogs went on to look for some more. We sat down to listen to the dogs. "When you get ready to go, let me know. We will have to call the dogs in. I can't leave them out here like I used to." Little John started talking about his wife's Rhode Island Red laying hens.

"The wife lets her hens out of the pen. They like to get out and scratch around the yard. When the coon dogs come in sometime in the morning after they have been out hunting all night, they will have them a chicken for a snack before bedding down to rest. That makes my wife mad so

I told her I would start putting up my coon dogs every night. She told me, 'If you want me to keep fixing your eggs for breakfast, you better do something, or you can start figuring out what's for breakfast. Because there are not going to be any eggs by the time those old coon dogs get through with my hens.' I decided right then I had better do something with those dogs. She is a much better cook than I am so I knew I had better listen to her. The other day I came home about midmorning. We had been out all night. When those old hens saw me pull up in my truck and unload those coon dogs, every one of those hens took off for the chicken pen. The last two that went through the gate, took their beaks, and pulled the gate closed so the dog couldn't get to them. That beat about all I have ever seen from a chicken."

About that time the dogs picked up another raccoon trail. They were really doing a lot of barking, but we never heard Missy.

Little John Looked at Willard and said, "Dad gum it!"

"We better get down there where Missy is. She has found the persimmon tree. You are not going to want to ride in the cab of the truck with her once she has filled up on fresh persimmons."

By the time we got down to where she was, we could hear her smacking one hundred feet away; she had already got her fill.

Little John said, "Well it looks like I will have to pour mineral oil down her tomorrow. Let's get them all together and head back to the truck."

"How are we going to get the dogs away from the tree that has the coon in it?" Willard asked.

"Oh that's easy," said Little John. "One thing these coon dogs like as much as treeing coons, and that is eating some of my wife's fried pork rinds. But don't tell Missy what they are. She can be a little bit sensitive."

Little John was right. When he opened that bag and the dogs got one whiff of the pork rinds, they all came running right on up to us.

"You better get you a handful of them before the dogs eat them all."

Little John was right.

"I think they were about the best pork rinds I had ever had," Willard said.

We got all the dogs and Missy to the truck and loaded them up. Missy started to jump in the cab when Little John opened the truck door. "Oh no, you're not riding up here, Missy," said Little John. "You will be riding in the back with the dogs, you old gas bag." Missy started squealing and jumped up in the back of the truck with the dogs. After getting everyone loaded up, it was a short drive back to the house to let me off.

Little John said, "It sure is good to see you, Willard. You remind me of your dad."

"I sure do miss that guy. I know you do too. Whenever you come for a visit, we will have to do this again. Thanks, Little John. This is just what I needed. It sure brings back a lot of good times and memories we have had. I will come back by to see you before I leave to go back to the city," Willard said.

CHAPTER 7

BETTIE JOE'S SURPRISE BREAKFAST

Willard thought everyone was asleep. When he walked in, Clare was still up. She was seating in her favorite chair by the window. "Well, how did that go, Willard?" Clare asked.

"It was a lot of fun. Just the way I remember it. When Little John is around, it is always fun. That pet pig Missy is amazing," Willard said.

"It's just not natural for a pig to run after coon dogs like that," Clare said.

Willard said, "I sure am missing that. I told Little John, and that I would come up as often as I can so he could take me coon hunting with Missy."

"Well, the acorn don't fall far from the tree. Your father sure liked going coon hunting with little John also," Clare told Willard."

"You know I don't know if I will be telling anyone back at the office about Missy. A pig that will tree a coon. I don't think they would believe me any way. That is something a person just has to see for themselves," said Willard.

"You know Mom. Just because a person may stretch the truth a little or a lot, it doesn't make them a bad person. That little John will do anything for anyone."

"He is what I call a good person," Willard said. "I better try to get some sleep as we have a big day tomorrow. We are trying out some new four row implements. Who would have ever thought you could make a tractor strong enough to plow four rows at a time?" Willard said.

"It's a good thing that you are doing for the farmers around here. Showing off those new big tractors. You know some of the farmers around here never go outside the farm and probably would have never seen what's out there. All this new equipment will make their farming a lot easier. Thank you for what you have brought for them to see," said Clare.

Clare slept in a little later the next morning after being up so late. When she went into the kitchen, it was 6:15 a.m. Bettie Joe had already had breakfast ready and Willard had already left. "Good morning. Sit down. I have made you eggs over easy, biscuits and sausage gravy, and fresh Folgers coffee. It's mountain ground you know," Bettie Joe said.

"Well, we live in the bottoms and are flatlanders but we can pretend that we are sating out on a big long porch overlooking the edge of the mountain where we can see down into a big valley," Clare said.

"Now we have to drink our coffee slow and sit back and enjoy it," said Betty Joe. "We need to go down to Polly's to pick up some supplies and start our cheese recipe."

After breakfast they got all the feeding done. Beverly was ready to be milked. "Beverly, are you showing off to

Bettie Joe? She gave two and a half gallons of milk. I don't know what we are going to do with all this," Clare said. "We have our five gallons of milk with the two and a half gallons we got last. If we use Frank's recipe, we have to get this cheese recipe figured out and soon. Or we will be swimming in milk around here."

On the way into town they crossed White Oak Creek, where they saw little Mickey Jones down by the bridge fishing. They moved in the old Miller farm back up the road. Clare stopped. "What are you fishing, for Mickey?" Clare asked.

"Catfish. I caught an eight-pounder yesterday. It was a flathead," Mickey said with excitement. Clare said, "Oh that's the best kind. I will give you two bits if you catch me one like that. We will be coming back though in about two hours."

"Well, I will sure try," said Mickey.

Mickey was a ten-year-old boy, but he looked like a grown man, very big for his age. He loved fishing and was very good at it.

They drove on down the road then went by Fred and Annie's house. They were farmers who were well known for their peanuts and watermelons they grew each year. Everyone said they grew the sweetest watermelons in the whole state. Everyone around the area looked forward to being the first ones to buy his watermelon each year. Annie was out by the road cutting some big beautiful pink flowers off a lilac bush when Clare stopped and asked, "Annie, do you have a cheese recipe? My old milk cow, Beverly, is giving so much milk, I am just throwing most of it away. I thought by making cheese I could make better use of the milk. It would be a lot better than seeing most of it go to waste."

"Yes, I used to make cheese, but have not made any since the kids were little," Annie said. "Little Kate could eat her weight in cheese if I set it down in front of her. You two make yourself at home. I will have to go in and look for it, and may take me a little while to find it. It has been a long time since I have seen it," Annie said. Clare and Bettie Joe walked over to where Fred was setting down in a chair under a big oak tree. Clare said, "Don't you have anything to do but sit here in the shade all afternoon?"

"Nope," Fred answered.

"You are going to get soft in your old age if you don't keep on moving around."

Fred just shook his head, looked over at Bettie Joe, and said. "That man of yours is really doing a fine thing for the farmers around here. Bringing all those new tractors and plows. Who would have ever thought a person could plow and plant four rows at a time? That will save the farmers so much time and money. That's real progress. I saw one of those super models and I kind of liked that red tractor. Poor Dobbin is getting old and so am I. All those long days walking up and down them long rows are real hard on a person. I have been thinking it may be time to start giving him a break from all that hard work. I think I would enjoy a break myself. I will still need him to pull my wagon because I can't drive a car and don't plan on learning," Fred said with a slight sound of relief.

Clare said, "Why you old lazy thing you. All that tractor is going to do is make you fat!"

"Putting on a few pounds may not be a bad thing," Fred said. "Then I could complain about my feet, knees, and back hurting."

About that time, Annie walked out with the recipe to make cheese. "I knew I would find it," she said.

Clare said, "Good thing you found the recipe when you did, cause this old man of yours is about to fall apart. Poor thing. Got bad knees, back, and feet."

Bettie Joe said they had better go.

"If we stay here any longer poor old Fred may just wither away to nothing right in front of our own eyes. We have five recipes now, and the way Beverly is giving milk right now we may have enough milk to try all of them by the end of the week. I will let you know how they turn out. Thanks so much, Annie. And Fred, don't sit out there under that old tree and fall asleep. You may fall out of that chair and break a hip to go with those bad knees and feet." Clare said.

Annie invited them all up for supper one night before Willard and Bettie Joe had to go back home. Willard and Fred were very good friends and always counted on each other whenever it was time to do any picking or hauling hay. They were as close as if they were blood kin.

Bettie Joe said to Clare, "You were a little hard on Fred."

Clare replied, "Oh that crazy old man, I have always talked to him like that. Even when Willard Sr. was alive Fred wouldn't have it any other way. If I was easy on him, he would think something was wrong with me. Fred and Annie are some of the kindest and most loving people in the whole valley, and they are like my brother and sister.

We have been through a lot of hard times together. I would not do anything that would upset them in any way. If you and Willard ever need something, you will find they are two people in the valley that will stand by you when everyone else is all gone. Are you about ready to try to make some cheese?"

CHAPTER 8

ONE RECIPE DOWN, FOUR TO GO

They made it to Polly's grocery store and went in. Clare started getting together the things she would need. About that time John the county agent came in and had seen Clare and Bettie Joe. John told Bettie Joe how proud he was of Willard for bringing the tractors and equipment to Cutter's Crossing for all the farmers to see. This made Bettie Joe and Clare feel very proud of Willard. John asked Clare if she had told them about her trip to the city last fall. Everyone around here was very proud of Clare. She had the best sweet potatoes in the whole county. I took her to a farmer's convention that was held in the State Federal building. She got to meet other farmers from all over the state.

"I have already seen some of the farmers here from the convention, and they were asking if you were going to be at the tractor demonstration," John said.

"I don't have any use for one of those tractors. I have Dan that can still pull a wagon and can still pull my one row cultivator. I don't have any interest in learning how to drive one of those big red things. Besides, Frank will do all my groundbreaking and any other plowing that I would need."

"Well, suit yourself. I hope the cheese comes out OK. I can't wait to try it."

"Polly has come up with a new cheese recipe for cheddar cheese. Maybe you can try this. Ralph, my cousin from out in Kentucky said that it's real popular up there. They like to put it on sandwiches. Make a batch and bring it in, and I will put in my cold case and I will serve it with some of that Petty Jean lunch meats on sandwiches. Let the people around here tell us if they like it or not. I think we have everything we need on this trip. We better get back home and get started on one of these recipes."

On the way back home they crossed the White Oak Creek, and little Mickey Jones was still down there fishing next to the bridge. Clare stopped and asked if he was having any luck catching any catfish.

"Sorry, Mrs. Bell, I have not caught anything yet. I am going to have to quit for the day and go back home to help dad feed the calves. Maybe I can come back and try again tomorrow."

"That will be fine. Just bring me the next big one you catch," said Clare.

They got back home middle of the afternoon, and Clare said, "Let's get Frank's recipe out, give it a try first. Frank's mother said five gallons of milk will make six pounds of cheese. You need two and quarter pounds of rennet. Put that in with your milk and bring to a boil for fifteen minutes. Take it off the stove, throw a towel over it then let it cool down until it is at room temperature. Get yourself a big wooden spoon and a bean pot lined with wax paper. Spoon it in the bean pot with the big wooden spoon, then cover it then put it in a refrigerator for three days. Take it out and dump it on a big plate and serve it with tomato soup, crackers, and some Petit Jean bologna. Now that sounds way too easy. There must be more to the recipe then that."

Clare looked at Bettie Joe who just shook her head as she never had mad cheese before. "The worst thing that could happen is that the cheese won't make, and I will have to feed it to the pigs," said Clare.

Betty Joe spoke up and said, "Well, we can't drink all that milk. And we have to feed it to them anyway."

"Let's cook it off and wait and see what happens," Clare said.

Bettie Joe made sure Clare stuck with the recipe. It didn't take long till they were waiting for it to cool down. That sure does not make any sense. Most things I try to make with a recipe is a lot harder to make than this.

They put it in the refrigerator for three days and then took it out. When Clare dumped it out on a plate, it broke the plate in four big pieces and felt like it would weigh at least twenty pounds.

Then Clare got a knife from the drawer and started to cut off a piece. "Oh my, I am going to need a bigger and sharper knife than that," Clare said. It was like a big thick chunk of rubber.

"Well, Bettie Joe, you may need to go out to the barn and get dads' old crosscut saw if we are ever going to cut this thing. I think I will call Frank on the party line. Let's see what he has to say about this. I think his mother was making tires for their wagons. He just thought it was cheese," Clare said to Bettie Joe.

Clare called Frank on the phone and he answered. Clare said, "I got your cheese recipe made for you to try out." "Oh it's good, isn't it?" Frank said.

"Oh yes, it sure is, Frank," Clare said.

"If you got strong teeth and jaws like a bulldog, you're going to need them if you eat this cheese."

"If it was black you would swear it could pass it for a rubber tire. I don't even think that my pigs will be able to eat this," Clare said.

"I sent Bettie Joe to the barn, and we are going to see if we can cut it with Dad's old crosscut saw."

The phone was real quiet on Frank's end. "Frank, you still there?" Clare said.

Then Frank spoke up.

"I don't understand it. Mom made it taste so good."

Clare said, "I know times where hard back then. You and your family must have been really hungry, if you ate anything that tasted like that! Now you come and get this thing, you can figure out what to do with it."

Bettie Joe and Clare got a big laugh after Clare hung up the phone with Frank. Bettie Joe said, "Strike one."

CHAPTER 9

❦

STRIKE TWO

"That's enough for today. We better get Willard's supper started as he will be home pretty soon," Clare said.

Clare met Willard at the door and said to Willard. "Just like old times. You still have a nose for getting home for supper before it gets cold."

"I could smell that all the way over at Joe Green's farm," Willard said.

"Get in and get washed up. Betty Joe and I just put it all on the table."

About that time they all sat down to eat. That was one thing that was very important to Clare. She always had supper ready, and she expected everyone to eat together. This gave all a chance to catch up on everyone's day and their needs. If you were not there, you just missed out on a good meal. And you wouldn't be getting a snack later. This was what Clare called bonding time. It kept everyone in the family close to each other's needs. They could talk about what they were going to do the next day, and if they were going to need any help with anything.

After supper everyone went out on the front-porch swing. It was a nice warm evening and very quite, just the sounds of some distant frogs out in the stock pond down below the barn and an old whippoorwill in the nearby forest singing. There was maybe a truck or car driving by going into town. We would sit out until everyone became sleepy, and then it would be time for bed. The day would start all over the next day. Clare said, "Tomorrow I need to go into town and get some sweet feed from the coop for Beverly. Bettie Joe, do you think your mother has any tips on cheese making?"

"I don't remember mother ever making any cheese, we never even ate it," Bettie Joe said.

"I think then, we will try John, the county agent's recipe. He seemed pretty excited about it. Let's see how it turns out," Clare said.

The next day they were up early. Willard had to show off some more of the new tractors. He was up early and on his way out, so Clare and Bettie Joe went out and got all the feeding and milking done in no time at all. Clare called Dan up. He was always ready to go to town. It was about 9:00 a.m. by this time. They got Dan hooked to the wagon and started up the road. About the time they crossed the White Oak creek. Mickey was already out there fishing. Clare looked at Bettie Joe and said, "For a ten- or eleven-year-old boy, he is sure interested in fishing."

Clare stopped and said, "Mickey, why are you fishing this early? Don't you have anything better to do?"

"I have been catching a lot of fish out here lately. I promised Fred and Annie I would bring them some catfish for supper tonight. They are going to pay me four bits. So I

114

wanted to make sure I have time to get theirs caught before it gets any later. I got to help Dad with the calves and don't want it to take me all day just to catch a few fish."

"Boy, you are quite the fisherman," Clare told Mickey. That made Mickey feel big and important coming from Clare. She was very important person in Mickey's eyes. It had just hit Mickey now that he had a title. If anyone asked he could tell them he was a fisherman.

"Well, keep up the good work, Mickey," Clare said.

And they drove on up the road to town.

After they got to the coop and went in, Little John and Missy, his pet pig, were in the coop. He was picking up a truckload of corn for his pigs. Bettie Joe had never seen Missy before, but she had already heard all about her from Willard. She walked over to Missy to say hi. Well, Missy took right up with Bettie Joe and started following her everywhere she went all over the coop.

"Looks like you have found a new friend," Little John said. "I still have one of her litter mates. If you want her you can take her back home to the city with you when you leave. It will be good for you to have her with you. She's pretty, looks just like Missy. She will remind you of home. In no time at all you could have her doing things around the house, and it will really surprise you how much she will be able to help you," Little John said.

"No thank you, but thanks for the offer."

Missy squealed real loud from what Betty Joe said.

Bettie went over to talk to her mother, Missy still following behind. By this time Missy was making her a little uncomfortable. Betty Joe's mother spoke up and said, "You have made a friend?"

Betty Joe smiled and said, "It is sure good being back in the coop. I sure miss work in here with you and Dad."

She told her mother how they were trying to make cheese and they were headed back to try once again. Clare had them load up the corn in the back of the wagon. "We best be on our way. Let's try again," Bettie Joe said to Clare. They said their good-byes and started back home. It was about noontime by this time. Clare got out John's recipe, and she and Bettie Joe started looking it over. They got all the ingredients together and started to see what would happen. This one said not to get the milk too hot, and it didn't say anything about putting it in an icebox for three days. Bettie said, "Well, let's see what it will do."

They went carefully by the recipe and waited to see if it would make. It never did get hard or any thicker than soup. "Looks like milk soup is we will call it," Clare said.

So the next day Clare called John at his office and told him about the trouble they had with the cheese recipe. John asked, "Did it come out pretty good?"

"If you like milk soup," Clare told John.

"Milk soup. That doesn't sound right," John said.

"Well, that's what we made with your recipe," Clare said.

Bettie Joe looked at Clare and said strike two. Two down and three more to go.

CHAPTER 10

WHAT WE CALL GOOD PEOPLE

Bettie Joe looked at Clare and said, "Thank you for letting me stay here and you taking the time to teach me about cooking. And this cheese making has been a real joy and a lot of fun. Well, let's get Ralph's recipe out. We'll give him a try. We should have enough milk for another run of cheese in the morning after we milk Beverly."

The next morning they were up and had all the feeding and milking done, and then it was time to try Ralph's recipe out. Well, this started out about like the rest of the other ones they did. Clare looked at Bettie Joe and said, "I don't know about this one either."

Bettie Joe said, "Let's keep it cooking so we can see what happens."

About that time the stainless-steel pot of milk and the other ingredients started boiling over the side of the pan and on top of the stove then onto the floor making a big mess. Clare was rushing around and fell flat on her backside. Bettie Joe reached to help Clare up and she fell. Willard had just came home and heard all the commotion in the kitchen. As he walked through the door, he fell flat on his face. Willard looked at Clare and said, "Well, are ya'll having a milk bath party?"

Bettie Joe looked at Clare and said, "Strike three, you're out! Willard, take this mess out to the pigs. Maybe they will get a laugh out of it too."

Willard took out what was left of the cheese to feed to the pigs and came back in to help clean up the mess in the kitchen. After getting everything cleaned up, Clare looked at Bettie Joe and said, "You know you are right. This cheese making is a lot of fun."

"I think we will have to wait about two days before we will have enough milk to try this cheese again. We could definitely use the break anyway," Clare said.

Willard said that they would be going back home at the end of the week. His company was going to be hauling back the equipment to the city starting tomorrow.

"Well, in that case let's try Bernie's recipe next. She said it was a keeper," Clare said.

Two days passed, and it was time to get out Bernie's cheese recipe and try it again. Bettie Joe read over the ingredients real close, and Clare tried hard to make this one work.

"This was perfect. The best cheese they had ever tasted. Those people up in Wisconsin know how to make their cheese," Clare said.

They were both very proud and ready to show some of it off. Clare said, "Let's take some down to Polly's grocery store so he can serve it with some of that Petit Jean sliced bologna and sandwich meats, or maybe some chicken loaf and crackers. That's what they did and everyone loved it. Polly couldn't keep it on the shelves."

Willard and Bettie Joe had everything ready to go back home. It had been a very good visit. This would be a visit that they would not forget for a long time. Clare picked up some measuring spoons and some mixing bowls. Polly had just ordered in some of those new electric mixers from his Sears and Roebuck catalog. Clare was the first to buy one for Betty Joe to take back with her. Willard took back with him something he had forgotten he had in him, and that was how deep rooted he was in Cutter's Crossing. Some people grow up and move away, and then the older they got the more they enjoyed coming back to see their families and where they came from. They knew one day they would be coming back to stay.

Bettie Joe took something back with her that she would be able to use for a very long time. Most of all she saw the caring and loving kind of people that the Bells were. Bettie Joe was very proud and glad for the most loving and caring family that she had married into. What Bettie Joe had seen in Willard's family was what she calls now, "good people."

STORY #3

ROB AND LARRY'S ADVENTURES

By Delbert Willcutt
Rob and Larry's Adventure
Cutter's Crossing Story Three
Written in May of 2013
Part of the Cutter's Crossing series

Written by Delbert Willcutt

CONTENTS

Summer with Rob and Larry

Introduction

This story is about two young boys who grew up playing together. They became friends and made memories and formed a bond that would last a lifetime.

Larry was a young black boy who lived down the road a mile or so from Rob.

This was the late 1950s, and it was a good time to be living in this farming town called Cutter's Crossing. Most people were sharecroppers, which means they worked off their part of the crop, and it was sold at harvest time. Some years were better than others. People were very happy living like this. It was a time when people worked together; they cared for one another and helped anyone if they needed it. It is good to be surrounded by good and caring people when times were bad. You could always count on a neighbor to pitch in and work together in those days.

These two boys learned how to become farmers while they were growing up in some of the best farmlands in the South.

Read this story about Rob and Larry and see if they are different than kids that you know today.

CHAPTER 1

KNOWING YOUR NEIGHBORS

Once there lived an old man named Paul. He lived with his wife named Lula. They called her Lou for short. Lou was like any other overprotective mother who loved her children very much and was always worried about them. One time Joe, her oldest son, said he had a stomachache and you would have thought he was about to die. She said, "Paul, this boy is wormy."

She held him down and gave him a tablespoonful of castor oil with a touch of turpentine; she would put just a hint of vinegar to make it go down easy. She would give it every day for a week. After that Joe was never sick again, and if he was he never let Lou know it. It would give you what we call around here the outdoor trots, which usually would last for about two to three days. We called it that because after you left the back door of the house and headed toward the outhouse, you had to trot to make it. The outhouse would sit at the end of the backyard away from the house. You would start out at a normal walk, but before you get to the outhouse you would be at an all-out trot. Sometimes you would make it and sometimes you wouldn't.

You see, Lou grew up in a time when you could not wait to see when someone got sick. Only how bad they were going to get.

They lived out in the country and it was a ways to town. If you needed a doctor there was one in town, and the doctor would do house calls. But Lou was the type that when it comes to her children being sick, she would try anything to get them feeling better as soon as possible.

One time Joe said he was bored and didn't have anything to do. He never made that mistake again because Lou put him out in the potato patch with a fruit jar and wooden tablespoon. He had to rake off the potato bugs into the fruit jar. After that he could always find something to do.

They loved living near this small town named Cutter's Crossing. This was during the late 1950s. It was a different time. In these days it seemed like about everything was done the hard way. You learned that sometimes it just takes a little longer to do things. Paul always said if he was going to do anything, it would be the hard way.

He just didn't know why. Maybe it was because he didn't know any other way. He was a poor farmer and had poor ways of doing things.

With not having the right equipment to work with, you learned to make do with what you had. Paul was in his sixties by now and was as strong as a young man, so he didn't back up from hard work. He loved it and liked how it made him feel after a long day of working in the fields. He would come in to a good hot supper, and then he liked to sit out on the front porch and watch the cars go by on their way into town. That's how he unwound after a hard day. After that a man could sleep well all night.

His son Joe would ask, "Dad, why would you break your back out in the field all day working so hard? There is an easier way of making a living."

Paul would say, "I like to eat and I always like to watch you and your mother eat. Farming gets in your blood. You are a farmer in good years and in bad years. You take whatever you get. Just be thankful for what you have."

There was not much work around there, so a lot of people moved up to the city and worked in the factories if they didn't want to become farmers. Paul never understood why his son moved up to the city to work in that factory. Chasing after that big money is what Paul would say. He may not make as much money right here working the farm, but it is all his to make. Farming is in his blood. I raised him that way. He just needs some time to figure it out.

Paul always said, "You can take the man out of the country, but you can't take the country out of the man." Paul longed for the day when his son would move back from the city and work the farm with him like they used to. Paul always thought this to himself as he didn't want anyone to know how much he missed having him around.

This was right in the middle of the best farmland in the South. It was good sandy-bottom land for as for as you could see around you. The land was easy to clear and to farm. This made the area around Cutter's Crossing popular for farmers to want to move in and farm it for themselves.

So their son Joe had a son and left him to live with Paul and Lou while he went up to live in the city where he worked in an automobile factory. The hours were very long, and for a ten-year-old boy like Rob there was just not much for him to do living in the city. Joe didn't have a wife. She left him after they moved to the city a few years back, and no one had heard from her for some time, so Joe wanted Rob to stay with Paul and Lou. He didn't want Rob to grow up living on the city streets. Joe knew he would get just what he needed and grow to be a fine young man there in Cutter's Crossing. Joe would come back and see him every few weeks or so.

Paul and Lou lived just out south of town about three miles. Rob was like any other ten-year-old boy, full of life and always into something. He had a knack for tinkering with things and liked to see how things were built or put together. Lou said he just liked to tear things up. His favorite thing to do was pull his wagon down to the city dump and see what people had thrown away. He would pick up old broken kitchen appliances and take them home and tear them apart to see if they could be fixed. Paul had to make a place in the barn, so he could work on his stuff. He had an old mule stall that he let Rob turn into a workshop. Paul had gotten a new tractor and didn't need the mule stall anymore, so he sold it. Paul thought this mule stall would work just fine as a workshop for Rob. Paul gave him a few tools to work with and helped him get it set up.

The old White Oak Creek was just down the road a little ways where Paul would take him to fish for some catfish for supper when Lou asked them to. Rob liked going down there and sitting on the bank of that old creek and listening to Grandpa talk and tell him stories about the past. It was times like this when he would be missing his father really bad, and Paul could take him down to the creek and then just a few minutes they would be laughing, and he wouldn't be missing his father anymore. For a ten-year-old boy, he was very big for his age and very strong. He was a lot of help to Lou and Paul, and they loved having him living with them. Whatever he was doing, he would drop it and come running if Lou would call him, because he knew if it was in between dinner or supper that would mean it was snack time. Maybe it would be a piece of pie that she would be baking for supper.

She knew he liked it better when it was hot and right out of the oven. Robert had an appetite like a full-grown man instead of a boy. But that was all right with Lou; she loved cooking for him. He could be out in his workshop; all she had to do was go out and hit a bean pot with a wooden spoon, and you would think he was about to tear the barn door off its hinges getting to the house. That boy just loved to eat Grandma Lou's cooking.

On down the road about a couple of miles lived a young black boy who was his age. They loved to play together. His name was Larry. His mother and father were sharecroppers who grew cotton down in the bottoms for a man named Bill Green. They lived in the Pine Hill community with a lot of their family and friends. They all worked as share-croppers. Larry's father drove a tractor and did all the plowing and planting for Bill Green.

In the fall when it was time to pick the cotton, they put all the cotton in a big wagon with tall sides on it after they picked it. We would get to ride on top of the cotton to the cotton gin. Larry's father would pull it with one of Bill Green's tractors. When it was time to pick the cotton, everyone around would come in behind the cotton picker and pick the cotton that it had missed. Those cotton pickers were amazing machines. It was like a huge vacuum that sucked the cotton off the stocks, and it would leave a little bit behind on the turn rolls, and if there were any trees out in the field the big machine could not get close to. All that would have to be picked by hand.

It seemed like what all people would talk about was getting all the cotton picked and how much they had picked that day. Then haul it to the cotton gin where it would be made into about a five-hundred-pound bale of cotton and then haul it to a cotton mill to be turned into cloth. It was early summer and school had just finished up for the year, which meant Larry and Rob would get to play for most of the summer.

Larry went to a small school in the Pine Hill community. The blacks didn't go to the regular public school. I never understood why. It was only four miles from town, and we had buses that went right passed their houses to pick up white kids on down the road. Larry and Rob were best friends. Rob didn't see Larry as being a different color, but only just like himself. Whenever you would see one of those boys, you would see the other one close behind. Paul and Lou knew Larry's mother and father really well. Grandpa Paul would buy pigs from them every year to fatten them out for winter's meat. They would call on Larry's father to help put up hay when it was time to put it in the barn, and if Larry's father needed any help with anything, Grandpa Paul was always ready to help out and any way he could.

It was middle of May, and even though it was spring, it was getting very warm. The spring of the year was very busy for farmers. They had to get everything planted if they were going to make a crop. After everything was planted in the ground, it was a big sigh of relief, and this gave Rob and Larry time to play.

Everything had bloomed out and turned green. Blackberries had bloomed, and it looked like there would be a big crop of berries this year if he could beat the birds to them. They liked to eat them as much as anyone else. Rob, he had his eyes on every patch of wild blackberries he could find along the fence row from his house to Larry's house. They would pick them and sell those down at Polly's grocery store in town. They could get twenty-five cents per gallon. This would keep them in soda pop and peanuts for a few weeks. They could buy two soda pops for ten cents each and a big bag of salted peanuts for five cents, and that would be enough for both of them to fill up their soda-pop bottles with those salted peanuts.

In these days it was a time when everyone knew everyone around Cutter's Crossing. Neighbors were willing to help out neighbors in any way needed. It was good to know that other people cared about you and your family and wanted to see you do well. This was during a time when you could count on your neighbors in a moment's notice.

Larry's mother was a midwife. She had delivered about all the children in the area. So sometimes Larry would have to go with his mother when someone was about to deliver. It was a lot of help to the expecting ladies in the area. It was four miles to town. If there were any problems with the delivery, Larry would be able to get the doctor in town.

Anytime Larry could take Rob along with him, he would. It was on a Saturday afternoon, and Larry came over to Rob's house to see if he wanted to go over to the Mrs. Keisha Carpenter's house. She was supposed to be delivering anytime. She already had eleven kids, so Larry said this should not take long. We should be able to leave within an hour tops. But after getting over to the Carpenters' house, most of the kids were out in the backyard playing a game of baseball. They wanted us to stay and play so it would even out the teams. This was always a lot of fun and time went by fast. In no time at all the baby came within fifteen minutes after we got there, and everything was just fine. Everyone lined up in one long line and went in and saw the baby and then back to the game.

Once you had seen one baby, they pretty much all looked the same to a ten-year-old boy. We were ready to finish up the game. But Mrs. Keisha and Larry's mother wanted us to see the new baby, after that everyone lost interest in the game, and it was time to go back home. The afternoon was just about over. Larry's mother on the way back home said, "Keisha makes my job easy. All I have to do is sit down in front of her and get ready to catch it." Rob and Larry looked at each other not fully understanding and knowing what all that meant. They just laughed right along with Larry's mom like they understood.

CHAPTER 2

PICKING UP TREASURES

One morning Rob got up early and went out to help Grandpa Paul do all the milking and feeding like he always did. He wanted to meet up with Larry, and they were going to the city dump to see what had been thrown away. It had been at least three weeks since they had been down to see what was there. He left and met up with Larry down at the bridge that went over the White Oak Creek. Larry was pulling a wagon that he had made with some hard rubber wheels and some pieces of wood he had picked up. From the last time they were down at the dump.

When they got there they made a big walk around to see if their was anything that looked different. That's when Rob spotted some bicycle parts. There must have been at least three parts of bicycles lying around there. They started loading them up on Larry's wagon. That's when they decided to go back home and see if they could make use of what they found.

When they got back home Grandpa Paul came out to see what they had found. The boys showed Grandpa the bike frames they had picked up.

Grandpa said, "Sorry, boys, looked like these frames are all broken right on the support rod that the seat is mounted on. Also these forks are as crooked as my Grandma Nettie's fingers. I think if you boys hold the support rod straight, maybe I can weld them back."

Grandpa had a welder that he used to weld up parts for his tractor if anything was broken. The neighbors would bring Grandpa Paul things that they needed to have fixed from time to time. He had one of the few welders in the area and was a very good welder. All three of the frames needed some welding; they were broken in one place or another.

"Grandpa, let's make it a little bit different," Rob said.

Then he drew on a piece of paper to show Grandpa what he meant. Rob said, "Let's put one frame on top of the other one. You're right, it will look a little different and be a lot taller."

"Just how are you going to get on it, to ride it?" Grandpa asked.

They got everything welded together and put the bike wheels on, and it was ready for a test drive.

Larry held the bicycle up so Rob could climb up on it.

"It rode like a dream," Rob said.

But it sure looked odd. There was one thing about Rob; he liked to be different.

"I know for one thing when you are riding this bicycle you will sure look different."

Grandpa said, "I don't get why you would want a bike like that, but it will be your elbows and knees that will be getting Skinned when you fall off of it."

Paul just shook his head and walked off and went back to working on the old hay rake that was by the big barn door.

They couldn't wait to take it down the old gravel road to see how it would handle on the loose gravel. They got back to the house when Paul asked, "Rob, how's it ride?"

"Well, it's a little frightening when I got going real fast. I got to thinking about falling on that gravel from this high up so I slowed down. I think I will be riding this bike a little slower than my other one," Rob said.

"That may be a good idea," Paul said.

The next day they couldn't wait to ride to town to show it off to their friends. Rob was up early to help with all the feeding and anything else that Grandpa Paul had for him to do. Paul knew what those two boys were up to. So he told Rob that he could do without his help for today if there was something he wanted to do. That was all Rob needed to hear. Rob was off like a flash to Larry's house. When Rob got over there Larry was out in the pig-pen helping his father put rings in the young pigs' noses that he had just wean off their mother pig. If they didn't ring their noses, those little pigs would be out faster than you could count to ten. They liked digging with their noses or rooting around the pen, is what Larry's father called it. If they got up next to the fence, next thing you would know they would be crawling under the fence, and there was now telling where they would be going from there. So ringing their noses would make it hurt when they rooted around.

But now if they were going to town, Larry would have to go down to White Oak Creek and jump in to wash the pig smell off him and his clothes. They had just started with the pigs, and there were forty-eight of them in five different litters, so that means that there are five different pens. Rob said, "Hey, can I help?" Then he jumped in to help. If you had never tried to catch some little eight-week old pig, well the more people you have in there, the better. If you were by yourself you could spend a whole day trying to catch them little things. After they get a little bit of mud on them, and they just slip right through your hands over and over again. By the time they finish up, the two boys were muddy from head to toe. They were so tired they could hardly stand up on two feet.

Rob said, "You know I don't think I want to ride the four miles into town after chasing those little pigs for the last four hours."

Larry said, "I was going to say the same thing. If you want to, just go without me. Let's go down to the white oak and take a swim."

They went straight as a string to the creek where someone had tied a rope to a limb that hung out about middle ways over the water. Larry was the first one to reach the rope swing. He grabbed the rope and made a big splash. Rob said, "That sure made you look a lot better, and I bet you smell a lot better too."

"Well, you should see yourself. Your Grandma Lou would not even know you," Larry said. It was amazing how cooling off in the creek made them feel so much better.

By this time it was late afternoon, so Rob went back home. When he rode his bicycle up to the house, he had to jump to get off and let the bike fall and hit the ground. He still hadn't quite thought of a way to get off or on it without help. He had been climbing up the side of the wooden rail fence next to the barn to get on. Paul saw Rob coming across the backyard and started slowing down and then fell over.

Paul walked over to Rob and said, "Rob why don't you ride alongside the fence next to the barn? You can get off and on the bicycle that way."

"I thank you are right," Rob said.

Rob was very proud of his newly designed bicycle. He knew he was the only one in town who had one like it. But this was going to be a bicycle that he probably would not ride every day.

CHAPTER 3

OLD LADY NAMED LINDA

After supper he went out to help with all the feeding and milking the cows. Grandpa Paul said, "What's wrong, Rob, you seem a little tired and slow."

Rob said, "I went over to get Larry to ride to town with me to show off the new bike. Well, his father had him catching little pigs that he had weaned to put rings in their noses. "There were five pens of them, he had forty-eight of those little pigs," Rob said.

"That took about all afternoon," Rob said. "I think I will be going to bed a little early tonight."

Paul laughed. "You must have gotten some mud on you. I noticed that your clothes were still wet when you got home. It is a good thing you washed that pigpen mud off you before your Grandma Lou seen you or smelled you like that."

Larry and I went to go down to Polly's grocery store. He had a new Sears and Roebucks catalog; it just came out. "It's the new summer edition," Rob said with excitement. They had new black-and-white TV sets that just came out with an outside antenna. They were guaranteed to have the best reception.

Rob still excited said, "Can we get one?"

"Well, I don't know," Paul said. "You need to talk with Grandma Lou about that."

"Let's see what she has to say about it," Paul explained. "Everything that goes into the house has to go through her, and anything that goes in the barn has to go through me. I stay out of her stuff, and she stays out of my stuff. This has worked for us for forty-five years, and I am not going to change that now."

"They have been talking all over town about TV shows that are airing right now. More and more people all over the valley are getting new TVs. This was keeping Polly pretty busy. If we could order it, we could have it in about two weeks," Rob said to Grandpa Paul.

"The next time we go into town we will have a look at them."

Rob agreed to come home early to help Paul weed the tomatoes after lunch. So he pushed his new bicycle invention up beside the wood rail fence to climb on, and off he went to Larry's house. When he got to Larry's he was sitting on the edge of the porch with his head down. He had a long switch in his hands; he had left some leaves on the tip of it. Well, Rob knew what this meant, so he never looked for a way off his bicycle easy. He just jumped off. Then he ran over and cut him a switch off a peach tree that was at the edge of the yard. He made the switch just like Larry's.

When Rob got over to the porch the fight was on. Larry had found a big red wasp nest just under the edge of the porch. He just started to fight them. This is one thing that boys liked to do to pass the time. If the nest was very big, you better have a switch in both hands. What you wanted to do was switch the wasps and knock them down and step on them. They will be some that will leave the nest, called scouts. Those are the ones you better watch out for, they mean business; they are coming to sting you. That is where the leaves on the end of the switch come in. You just want to shoo one or two off the nest at a time. Sometimes you would get more wasps off the nest, then you could fight, and that would be when you would probably get stung. If they manage to sting you, the wasps had won the fight and they beat you. To be fair to the wasps you should leave the nest and try again another day.

Rob got stung on the back of the hand. Larry laughed and said you have got to be quicker than the wasp. Then they walked back to their bikes, hopped on, and started riding down the road to town.

This ride went fast; they were in town in thirty minutes. Just as you get to town if you turn right on Maple Street and go a few blocks and then left on Ash Street, this would take you to the back of Polly's grocery store. Most of the time they would cut across old lady Linda's backyard. She had a corner lot that was about two or three acres. She lived in a big old two-story wood-frame house that was a little rundown; well, a fresh coat of paint would not hurt it. But she keeps her garden and her shrubs and plants around her house always groomed and trimmed and looking good. They could save some time by going across her backyard.

It took them from Maple Street to Ash Street. If she didn't see them, everything would go pretty good. But if she did, well it could get pretty bad before you could get across the yard and out on Ash Street. Linda, she was a little dried-up old lady. She didn't have any teeth, and she dipped sweet Garrett snuff all of the time she always had a little bit of snuff that would leak down the left side of her mouth, or maybe it could have just been a stuff stain. I don't really know. She talked low and slow and had a whistle that came after each sentences. That sounded a little odd but interesting.

It happened this day that she was in the backyard and had seen the boys coming though at the back of her garden. She had an old mutt dog named Bert. He was half beagle and half weenie dog or something. So she hissed old Bert on us. Well, with only three-inch-long legs poor old Bert could not run very fast. Bert's bark was lot worse than his bite. Bert wasn't much of a problem; he was easy to get away from. One thing we had to watch for was that she could throw a rock real hard and straight for an old lady in her late seventies. All those years as a child she must have had to hunt rabbits with rocks because she didn't have a shotgun.

But she stayed in good practice throwing at rabbits or squirrels when they would come up to eat from her garden. Lucky for Larry he made it across the yard and though the ditch and on the road before Linda hit him. But as for Rob, riding on that big tall bicycle made him a better target. She hit him three times before he could make it up on Ash Street. Every time she would throw, she would holler GET OUT OF MY YARD! By the time Rob got out on Ash Street, he was crying like a five-year-old kid. Larry was laughing so hard he had fallen off his Bike and was lying on the side of the road. Rob fell off his Bike and landed in the ditch beside Larry on the edge of road and started to check on his wounds where he had been hit by the gauntlet of rocks Mrs. Linda had thrown at the boys.

Rob was still sobbing and looked at Larry and said, "We need to start just riding on up the street instead of cutting across Mrs. Linda's yard. For an old lady she sure can still throw really hard."

Larry had to help Rob on his bikes, and the two boys went on down the road to Polly's grocery store and ran in. Larry's father had given them twenty-five cents each for helping him ring the pigs' noses the day before. They bought a big grape soda each and a big bag of peanuts to share.

Polly asked the boys what they were up to. Then they asked Polly if they could look at his new Sears and Roebuck catalog.

They went over to the table where the old men would be normally playing dominos, but today none of the old men were in the store. So they had the whole table to themselves. It didn't take them long to find the black-and-white TV sets; they had them at all different prices. So after reading up on them as much as they could, they would be able to tell Grandma Lou all about them and how much they would cost.

CHAPTER 4

❧

TOO CLOSE TO CALL

Rob and Larry went out on the bench that sat on the sidewalk next to the building to finish their soda and peanuts and were just about to leave when a boy from school came by the store. It was Joey from Rob's fourth-grade class. He had seen Rob's oversized bike and asked, "Rob, how did you make this bike and why? Isn't it hard to get on?"

"No, not if you have a fence to climb on or a sidewalk bench to stand on," Rob said.

"It looks really neat. Can I ride it?" Joey asked.

"Sure," said Rob.

"Just don't go too, fast you may crash. And it's a long way to the ground, and I don't want to see you get hurt, Joey," Rob said.

Well, Joey got up on the sidewalk bench and climbed on, and then took off down the sidewalk. He went down to the stop sign, turned around, and started back down the same way he came back to Polly's store.

On the way back he passed Sal's Beauty Shop just as Jenny Crabtree was coming out. She was so busy looking at her fancy hairdo in the reflection in the storefront window and didn't see Joey on the big bike.

There was a big open-top trash can just to the right of the door. About the time she saw Joey, he tried to miss her and took to the street.

Jenny spun around and fell back in the trash can.

Now all that work she had done putting her hair up in a beehive hairdo, all the hair on top of her head fell down in her face and looked like she had grown some long bangs.

Jenny was a true redhead; well, now her face was as red as her hair.

She went to a lot of trouble getting all fixed up for dinner out with her husband. She was hollering so loud, it sounded like Little John's coon dogs when they had treed a coon.

Joey headed back to where the boys were still sitting on the bench. Joey rode up beside the sidewalk bench and got off and said, "Rob, it rides really good, I got to go."

Well, when Jenny had finally figured out what had happened, she looked down the sidewalk, and all she could see was me and Larry. Her standing there with her hair down in her face and what looked like a piece of candy wrapper stuck to the back of her good clean dress.

Grandpa Paul always said if you are ever out in the forest and come up on a wild animal don't run, just stand still.

Well it was kind of like that. I think if we would had turned and ran she would have run us down like we were little mice.

We were afraid to leave so we just stood there and let her holler it all out.

She finally gave us one last hoot and stomped her feet and shook her fist and turned and went back into Sal's beauty shop.

Larry looked at me and said, "Now she's really mad. We better leave before she comes back out."

Rob and Larry jumped on their bikes and headed for home. When they rode past Mrs. Linda's house, she was out in the front by the road weeding a flower patch.

But they were not even thinking about crossing her yard and having to face rapid rock fire again. When they passed by, Rob looked at Mrs. Linda. She was smiling.

It didn't take them very long, and they were at Rob's house. Larry stopped and went in with Rob to talk to Grandma Lou about the black-and-white TV sets. Rob was so excited Grandma Lou had to tell him to slow down and stop talking so fast.

Rob asked, "Can we order one? Polly said we can have it in two weeks."

"We will talk about that at supper tonight, with your Grandpa Paul," Lou said.

Rob and Larry went out to the barn to play for a while before Larry had to go home. They found some bumble-bees flying around the barn and picked up some flat piece of wood and started swatting at them. This would keep them busy for a while or until one of them got stung. Then it would all be over; the bees would be the winners. It was getting late afternoon, and Larry had to go home for supper. Larry said his good-bye and rode his bike on down toward his home.

Well, the suspense of waiting until supper to find out if they were going to get a TV set or not was very exciting for Rob. All kinds of things were running through his mind. He had the perfect set picked out if he could get Grandpa Paul talked into buying it. Lou called everyone to the table to eat supper. Rob was the first one to sit down at the table. Lou said, "Now, Rob, I don't want to hear anything about the TV until everyone has eaten their supper." Rob was so excited he could hardly eat anything, and it seemed like it took Grandma Lou a very long time to finish eating.

"OK, Rob, what do you have on the TV sets from Polly's store?" Paul asked.

"The Sears and Roebuck catalog has a twenty-inch black-and-white Magnavox for 249.50. It's the top of the line, Grandpa," Rob said. "Or you can get a General Electric twenty-one-inch black and white for 149.95? They are running a special on the General Electric this month. You get a free outside antenna with it if you order before the end of the month."

"That's a lot of money, Rob. If you asked your dad to go half, we will go half for the General Electric."

Rob jumped up and ran for the party line to give his dad a call. He was coming Saturday for a visit so Rob wanted to make sure he had the money to place the order from Polly's store.

Well, everything was set and looked like Rob, Grandpa, and Grandma Lou was going to be the new proud owners of a twenty-one-inch General Electric black-and-white TV set. Rob was going to tell them about the new color TV set that has just come out, which was only five hundred, but he thought he would just keep it to himself. The black and white will be just fine.

CHAPTER 5

FINE-TUNING A TV

After getting the new black-and-white TV set ordered down at Polly's store, the next two weeks went by real fast. Rob went down about every day or two to see if the TV had been delivered yet. Finally it came. Rob and Larry had been at Polly's store. Polly told Rob that the TV was here, and Rob could pick it up anytime. So Larry and Rob rushed home to let Grandpa Paul know that it had been delivered. On the way back home the boys started to cross Mrs. Linda's backyard to save time when they saw Mrs. Linda out in her tomato patch with an elm switch walking up and down the rows hollering and slapping the ground around the plants. That seemed a little strange so they stopped to watch to see what was going on.

Linda was throwing up her arms, jumping up and down. Larry looked at me and said, "I wonder what kind of fit is that? I have never seen anyone act like that before."

Rob said, "Let's watch her and see what she will do next."

About that time Linda had seen the two boys sitting on their bikes, watching her.

Linda said, "What's the matter, have you boys not ever seen someone switching their tomatoes before?"

Larry looked at Rob and said, "Why would you switch your tomatoes?"

Rob hollered back at Mrs. Linda and asked, "Why are you switching your tomatoes?"

"That's so they will get to growing," Mrs. Linda said real slow.

The two boys shook their heads and rode on down the road.

Rob looked at Larry and said, "That is one strange lady. You know I think she should start threatening them with rocks instead of a switch, because she sure is awful good at throwing them."

"Yes and she can hit what she aims at, and you have the marks to prove it," Larry said.

When they got back home, they told Grandpa Paul that the TV set was in and sitting down at Polly's store.

"Well, let's load up and go get it before it's too late to hook it up."

Lou said, "She had heard on the party line that *Gun Smoke* was coming on at seven o'clock tonight. She had heard Cathleen Jones talking about it. That James Arnest was one tough lawman from Dodge City Kansas." He was sent there to get rid of all the outlaws in that part of the country. He is a United States Marshall.

Well that sounded like something Grandpa Paul would like to watch. Everyone was excited about picking up the TV set, and hurried down to Polly's store.

When they walked in it was sitting by the back door in a big box and a smaller box next to it. "Is that the antenna?" asked Lou.

"Yes, and all the directions are right in the boxes and very easy to follow. I didn't have any problem getting mine hooked up and ready to watch," Polly said.

They loaded it up and hurried home to try their luck with the directions. Lou read all the directions out to Rob, Larry, and Grandpa Paul. They got the antenna up and wire pulled through the window and hooked to the back of the TV set. And then they were ready to turn it on, they plugged it up, turned it on, and got nothing but what looked like snow. You couldn't make out one single thing.

Grandma Lou said, "You have to turn the antenna until it comes in clear is what it says here in the directions." Grandpa went out to turn on the antenna, and Rob stood at the door, and Lou hollered out when to turn the antenna. Turn, turn, stop, finally got a picture that you could tell what it was. Paul come running back in the house to see what looked like two men riding horses in a snowstorm. Lou said, "It was better than that one minute ago so go back out and turn it again." Well, Paul could tell that having a TV set may not be all it was cracked up to be, if all that he would get to do was turn the antenna. And about that time Rob said, "Turn it slowly."

"Stop!" Lou said to Rob, who was standing at the door.

"It's perfect," Grandma Lou said.

Paul shook his head and came into the house, just in time to see *Gun Smoke* go off the air. Paul said, "I can see that watching TV is going to be a three-person job. One to watch, one to stand at the door and holler, and one to turn the antenna."

"Well, maybe next Saturday night I will be able to watch the whole show."

"Rob, I am going to show you how to turn the antenna," Paul said.

It didn't take long to get the TV set tuned in, and it was coming in pretty plain. Paul got into the house in time to see the *Jackie Gleason and the Honeymooners*. He was a big, loudmouthed man who lived in the city and drove a city bus; it was a very funny show and a lot of fun to watch.

CHAPTER 6

ROB AND LARRY'S
FISHING LESSON

They stayed up late watching the new TV set, until it went off the air at twelve midnight. Everyone was still up at 6:00 a.m. the next morning but moving around a little slow. Paul said, "We can't be staying up so late watching the new TV set when we have so much to do the next day. Frank is coming over today to cut the hay meadow down below the barn, and if it dries out tomorrow we will rake it and bale it."

Rob said, "I will need your help putting it in the barn."

Paul said, "So you and Larry will have to stay apart for one day, unless he wants to make six bits by helping you stack the hay in the barn."

Rob said, "Larry and I are going down to White Oak Creek to catch some catfish for supper tonight, and I will ask him if he wants to help out."

After getting all the feeding done, it was midmorning, and Larry came over to play and he had an old Zebco fishing reel that he had found at the city dump and it seemed to work still pretty good. He didn't have a rod for it so we used some of Grandpa's baling wire and tied it to a cane pole. We threaded some pieces of wire though the cane pole to make some eyes for the string to pass through. It looked great. All that was left to do was to go down to the creek and try it out.

They went out to the workshop and got a pail for worms and headed to the creek. It was not a problem to find fish bait; all you had to do is rake back leaves under some trees on the creek bank, and you could find all the worms you could need in just a few minutes.

The boys tied their hooks and a bobber on the line, and they were fishing in no time at all. Larry's makeshift cane pole rod seemed to be working and was holding up pretty well. They were not having much action on their line so they decided to throw some rock in the water, to see who could make the biggest splash. About that time on down the creek bank they saw Little Mickey Jones from the fifth-grade class. He was fishing for flathead catfish. Mickey knew all the good fishing holes up and down the creek and knew just how to catch the big fish. Mickey was an eleven years old and very big for his age. He had muscles like a grown man and was as strong as a young bull calf. He always had a big caw of tobacco in his mouth when he would be fishing. Mickey said, "You have to spit on your hook for good luck if you want to catch the big ones." It must have worked pretty well for him, because it was like he could look down into that old muddy creek and see right where the big catch fish were lying. Then all he would have to do is drop his line down, and he could catch one every time.

"If you are going to catch any fish, you have got to stop playing in the water and making so much noise. You are scaring all the fish to the other side of the creek," Mickey said.

Well, it sounded like Mickey knew what he was talking about. After all he had the reputation of being a good fisherman, and Rob and Larry were just beginners. After they got quiet and stopped making so much noise, they started getting bites of their own. Larry or Rob hadn't caught anything yet when Mickey said, "It's not so much as how much bait you have on your hook. It's how you make it look to the fish. If you want the fish to bite you have to make them think if they don't bite the hook you are going to take it away from them, and then they will surely bite the hook. Then all you have to do is set the hook and pull them in."

Well, after heeding Mickey's fishing tip, in no time at all both of the two boys had fish on their lines. They were not as big as the fish that Mickey was catching, but Mickey said, "Rob you will catch a lot more little fish then big fish. That's just the way fishing works out."

In no time at all they had caught all the fish they needed for supper, with the three fish that weighed six pounds that Mickey put on the stringer. By that time it was late afternoon, and it was time to go home. Rob and Larry divided the fish up, and Larry took half home for their supper that night.

When Rob came in with all the fish he had caught, Grandma Lou was very impressed, she took one look at the fish and said, "Well, you better get to cleaning them if you want to have them for supper tonight."

Grandpa Paul came out from the barn and Lou said, "You too. Better get to clean these fish if you want me to cook them."

Paul said, "Let's get to it, Rob, this is a nice catch for an afternoon."

Rob had worked up a big hunger, and for a ten-year-old boy Grandma knew just what kind of an appetite he would have, so she cooked all the fish he had. Rob went out and cut a big head of cabbage out of the kitchen garden to make some coleslaw with green onions and corn bread with sweet tea, so this made up a big pile of fried fish, and everyone had all they could eat. After supper everyone went out on the front porch to sit and watch the cars going down the road on their way to town and sit down on the parch swing and talk. Grandpa would tell stories of when he was young, how things were done in the good old days. This was the way Grandpa Paul would tell it.

"Everything was done the hard way, or it wasn't done," Grandpa would say. "We had to go to school in a one-room schoolhouse. Walked to school uphill both ways, rain, snow, or sunshine."

Paul would always say that he preferred the sunshine.

"Rob, you are very lucky to be living in the day you are living in with all the new inventions to make things more profitable and easier. Who would have thought that now you could buy six roll equipment that would fit on your tractor? A farmer can work six rows at a time, that's amazing. Now think of the fuel and time you save. You should be able to live a long time, you even get to ride a bus to school," Grandpa Paul said with a smile.

Grandma Lou said, "Let's go in and get ready for bed. The mosquitoes are about to eat me up."

It had been a long day and that sounded like a good idea.

CHAPTER 7

❧

LLOYD TURNER

Grandma Lou's radio that she kept in the kitchen had stopped working. She liked to listen to the daily soaps while she was cooking or canning. Grandpa Paul asked Rob if he wanted to go down to Lloyd Turner's house with him to see if he could fix the radio. Paul knew he was a very interesting man and that Rob might like to meet him. He thought all that stuff may be fascinating to Rob.

Rob had an old washing-machine motor he had been working on that needed some motor brushes and a new cord. Paul knew that Lloyd would have what Rob would need to get his motor running. Lloyd was a good friend of Paul's for a long time. He was a handyman that people would use to do odd jobs. That Lloyd, he could fix about anything he set his mind to.

Lloyd was very curious about things and how they worked. He could spend hours, even days, tinkering with something. If he couldn't fix it, he would scrap it out and would never give up and throw it away.

If you ever needed him, he was never hard to find. All you needed to do was go out at the local city dump site.

If he wasn't there, he would be at his house working on something.

Anytime someone would throw something away that was broken, he would take it home and try to repair it. It was amazing how much stuff people would throw away that just needed a little fixing. He had been finding things out at that dump site for years and would bring them home to fix them. You know sometimes after cleaning, fixing, and replacing parts that needed replaced, when he finally got something fixed, you could not tell it from a brand-new one.

He had so much stuff at his house that you couldn't walk through it, or find a place to sit down, in the whole house. Even outside of his house was such a mess that you couldn't even tell what color of paint the house was.

If you asked him if he had something, he could find it in a minute. It was amazing how he could keep up with everything in all that mess.

He liked to talk about the future, if you hung around very long. The more you stayed and listened to his story, the stranger he would get. He would start off and tell the same story every time, if you would let him. It was very strange and the longer and more into the story he got, the more frightening the story would get. He would say the stars would line up in a straight line. Then that's when fire-balls would rain out of the sky, as big as one of those compact cars.

It would make the hair on the back of your neck stand up just listening to Lloyd tell his story. That is what Paul would say. Lloyd would say all of this stuff around here looks likes junk to most people, but it will become very valuable someday.

Grandpa Paul said, "That sound a little strange for a man to act and say some of the things he would say, but only time will tell. So Paul would just agree with him and get out as soon as the story's got hard to take.

A few years later, he came up missing and no one had seen him for some time. We heard people say he just packed up a few things in a back pack took off walking down the road.

Lloyd Turner just walked off from everything. No one knew why, he said he wasn't going any were special; he just wanted to see some country he had never seen before. Grandpa Paul said, "A man sometimes just needs to work out his problem in his own way. You know, after a while, the city found out about his death."

He didn't have any family around that anyone could find. So the good people of Cutter's Crossing went in cleaned up his house and had an estate auction.

News traveled fast around the state, and a lot of collectors came from all over when they found out about all his antiques appliances and rare pieces.

Some of the things sold for thousands of dollars. All the money that the auction brought in was a lot more than anyone expected. All the money went to the local church where he attended from time to time. And the city for some much needed improvements to their City Park. They put a big sign up and called it Turner Park, and even renamed the city street that lead to the park off the main road, to Turner Street.

So after that the church bought a statue of an old man setting at a table working on a clock, in memory of Lloyd Turner. The man at the table looked a lot like Lloyd the only thing was different was who ever made the statue didn't put a hat on his head. He always wore a St Louis Cardinal's ball cap. That was his favorite baseball teams name. He always had its bill turned up in front, it looked strange, but I guess that was the most comforting way for him to wear it. I never saw him without a hat on his head, unless he was going to church.

The good people of Cutter's Crossing thought this way he would never be forgotten for what he did for the town. He will be missed around here for a long time. He had helped a lot of people, around the valley if they needed something and couldn't pay for it he would help them out for free. He would say you pay me next time this one was on me. That's why everyone likes to have him fix things for them. He never had to look for work and this would always keep him busy. He would say," When you help someone in need, it will always come back to you". Rob got what he needed to fix his washing machine motor, Grandma Lou got her ratio fix and they went on there way.

CHAPTER 8

GOING TO THE
LIVESTOCK AUCTION

The next morning everyone was up early and ready to get the day started. It was Saturday and Larry's father was going to taking some pigs to the local livestock auction to be sold. Rob was telling Grandpa Paul, "Let's go with them. I hadn't been in a while and you never have. It will do you good to see what the farmers do with their animals when it's time for them take them to the market. It should be a very interesting day for you."

They went over to Larry's father's house to give them a hand catching the little pigs. When they are small pigs to catch a few extra hands always comes in pretty handy. Those pigs can slip right through your hands over and over again.

One or two people could spend a half of a day to do what four people could do in just a little while when it comes to catching small pigs. This was very entertaining to see two young boys and two grown men trying to catch a few small pigs. It still took a little longer than one would think.

By the time the last one was loaded up, everyone was pretty tired of running around the pigpen. They all got cleaned up and were ready to leave for the livestock auction.

This was almost noon so when they got to the sale barn, they got the pigs checked in and then went back to Polly's grocery store for some lunch. Paul had his liver loaf sandwich with mustard and a slice of tomato. Larry and I had bologna with cheese with mustard and lettuce. Larry's father had chicken loaf with cheese mustard lettuce and tomato.

They sat out on the bench out on the sidewalk because coloreds were not allowed to eat inside with the white folks ;it was just the way things were then.

That Petit Jean brand meats has got to be the best lunch meat money can buy, Paul said. They had just sat down, and Paul looked at Rob and he was licking his fingers.

Paul and Larry's father, had just taken one or two bites from their sandwich. Paul said, "You two may as well go back in and get another one. We don't want to hear your stomach making noises all during the auction."

Larry's father asked Paul, "Didn't you feed him breakfast this morning?"

This was a big deal for all the area farmers and ranchers to come to the local livestock auction. There would always be some kind of entertainment; most of the time the young calves had never seen anything outside of their pens and fences.

So when they came to town they were not very happy and would jump out of the trucks or trailers that they were brought in and then running lose all over town, or until someone could catch them. Sometimes it would be like the running of the bulls like they do in Spain; half the town would be out trying to catch the young calves.

If they got them back to the sale barn that would be entertaining just to watch them try to run the people out of the pen where they were. It didn't matter if it was up and out over the top of the pen that they were in. This was a lot of fun to watch to see who was going to make it over the pen, first the calves, or the man who was trying to pen them.

It was almost time for the sale to start so we went in and got a good seat about middle ways up.

Rob asked, "Can't we sit down by the fence?"

Those sets are empty.

"No," said Grandpa Paul, "when the sale starts you will see why."

About that time the auctioneer came out and got a microphone and started to start the sale. "He could talk faster than anyone I have ever heard before," Rob told Larry. But you know I can't understand a single word he is saying. About that time they started to sell chickens, ducks, and turkeys. Then there were goats, and after that horses and mules.

Finally the little pigs, before they brought them in to sell, the auctioneer stopped the sale, and asked little John if he would take Missy his pet pig out until all the pigs have been sold.

Little John was a pig farmer that lived out east of town and always had his pet pig Missy with him everywhere he would go. She would get a little sensitive and start squealing as loud as she could when the pigs started coming through the arena to be sold.

Little John tied a grass-string rope around her neck, that he always carried in his back pocket, and took her out to the truck until all the pigs had been sold.

After that the young calves came through; that's when it made sense to me why no one was sitting in the seats down front next to the rails around the arena fence. It was early summer, and the grass still had a lot of water in it and that's what calves eat the most of. So anyone setting in the front row would need to go straight home after the sale and take a bath. They would have a combination of greenish brown all over them.

This was all afternoon watching all the livestock sale When it was over we went outside, and some little calves had gotten out of someone's truck, and two teenage boys were chasing them all over town, trying to catch them but without a pen to run them in, it made it a little tough. One of the boys got close enough to get a rope on one of them, but it didn't take the calf long to lose the boy, and now it was dragging the rope behind. About that time Mickey Jones came out of Polly's grocery store and saw the young calf dragging the rope and ran over, grabbed the rope, and the calf came to a stop. For a young boy only eleven years old, he was as strong as a full-grown man. So Larry and I ran over and got behind the calf, and Mickey dragged the calf over to the sale barn and put him in a pen. The man at the back of the sale barn told Mickey, "You want to make two dollars, you catch the other one and bring it to me."

The man handed Mickey the rope back, and off the three boys went to look for the other calf. This made and interesting afternoon. You know it wasn't long, and Mickey had the other calf hemmed up in an alley behind Betty's café and had it caught in no time. Mickey gave Larry and Rob one of the dollars; it didn't take us long to think what to do with fifty cents each. We all went to Polly's store for soda pop and peanuts.

After that, Larry's father picked up his check for the young pigs he had sold, and it was time to go home. Rob looked at Grandpa Paul and said, "Going to the livestock auction is a lot of work but a lot of fun."

Larry's father let Grandpa and Rob out at their house. Grandpa Paul thanks them for a fun-filled afternoon and said, "We will do it again real soon."

CHAPTER 9

HAIRCUT FOR LARRY

Grandma Lou was just finishing up with supper and getting everything set on the table, as Paul and Rob came through the back door. Rob was the first one to sit down at the table and Lou asked, "Rob, have you washed up?" "Sorry," Rob said, so Rob jumped up and ran for the sink where Paul was still washing his hands when Rob came in and tried to push his way to the sink so he could get cleaned up and get started eating. After supper they sat down in front of the TV set to watch *Gun Smoke*. Grandpa Paul had waited all week to see James Arness the big lawman at Dodge City. He wanted to see if he was as tough as everyone had said he was. He still hadn't gotten a chance to watch the program yet, and it had been the talk of the town.

The next morning everyone was up and ready to get the day started. After finishing up breakfast, Grandpa Paul and Rob went out to feed the animals. Paul wanted to get started working on a pump motor that he used to pump water out of the stock pond for irrigation. Rob wanted to go to town with Larry; it was time for Larry's haircut.

Over in the southern part of town, what everyone called box town, there was a barbershop where all the coloreds would get their haircut. And it was a lot of fun going in to see Joseph the barber; he would always pick on us from the time we came in the door until we left. There was a man in there named Tyrone Carpenter; they called him TC for short. He would always tell stories; he had to be the best storyteller ever. He would throw up his hands get up out of his chair and walk around, and he made you feel like it was real and you was right there. But at the end of the story it was always turned out to be not true.

On the way they wanted to go by Polly's grocery to look at the new Sears and Roebuck catalog. When they went by Mrs. Linda's house, she had a big steel pot with a fire built under it. There was smoke raising way up in the sky and you could see the smoke from a long way off. She was standing next to it with a big wooden stick and stirring it. Larry looked at me and bugged out his eyes. Larry asked Rob, "What is she doing now?"

"I think she must be making some kind of potion," Rob said. "We better keep our eyes on her to see what come from this."

All kinds of things ran through those two little minds. They stopped on the side of the road and started watching her. About that time Mrs. Linda turned around and saw the two little boys watching her. She looked at Rob and smiled. Larry looked at Rob and his eyes bugged out. About that time Bert saw the two boy and started across the yard barking. Larry said, "We better get going." They jumped on their bikes and hurried on down the road to Polly's grocery store.

When they got to Polly's store, they went in and asked if they could look at his Sears and Roebuck catalog.

Polly said, "You two boys are about to wish my new catalog to pieces. And yes you sure can." Polly smiled.

They stayed for a while until they had thumbed through about half of it. Then Larry said, "I need to go get my haircut." So they were off to Joseph's barbershop. "I sure hope TC is there," Rob said. When they got there and went in there were three people ahead of Larry so they would have to wait their turn. This was just fine because TC was in, and it would give him time to tell them a story.

TC was setting over by the window reading a fishing magazine. The two boys walked over to TC and asked, "How are you doing?"

TC was an old man, must have been in his late seventies by now. He said, "I just got back from up north fishing the Big Piney River for brown bass. You know the funniest thing that happened to me while I was fishing?

I had my waders on. We had just got a big rain the day before. The water was up a little. I must have lost track of how far I had waded up the river, when I saw a big black bear on the bank looking right at me. You boys know those things can swim really well a lot better than I can. I had to think what I was going to do. I couldn't outswim him. I was too far to my truck to try to get out of the water and make a run for it. I know for a fact if I could make it to the bank I was scared enough that I could easily outrun him. But I couldn't remember how far it was to my truck. Now, boys, I am not as young as I used to be. I can still run pretty fast, but I can't run as far as I used to. I had a nice brown bass in my bag so I tossed it too him. Well, that old bear ate it in two bites. That was all I had, so I knew that I better get to fishing. So I turned back toward the truck and started throwing line. He was following me back down the river. About that time he stood up on his back legs and let out a big growl. That's when I caught another fish. I hurried up, took it off my line, and tossed it to him up on the bank and went back to throwing line.

Two bites, it was gone. I thought if I was going make it back to my truck, I had better get to catching big fish as fast as I could, so I could fill him up."

Rob and Larry were getting really caught up in the story, both of their eyes bugging out of their heads and them sitting on the edge of their seats.

"I needed to get in some deeper water to catch bigger fish. I stepped off in a deep hole of water. The water, it went up to my chest. Cold water started running down into my waders. But I couldn't let that bother me. I had to catch fish to keep that bear from having me for a snack. I looked over on the bank. He was still there looking right at me and waiting on another fish. Finally I caught another one that I tossed up to him. He took three bites on this one, and I thought maybe he was getting full. I could see the truck just ahead. I thought if I could catch one more maybe it would be enough to keep him busy until I could get to the bank. It took four throws before I caught another one. It had to be at least a three pounder. I took it off my hook and tossed it to him. That's when I thought I better get out of the water and make a break for the truck. About the time, I started up the riverbank and started to run. He stood up on his back legs, and that's when I heard him make another big growl. I turned around and looked at right at him. He was on the other side of the river from me. That's when I noticed him raising one of those long arms up and giving me a big wave. I knew right then that I had just made me a friend. Well, that old lazy bear didn't want to get in the water and get wet catching his own fish for his supper. He wanted me to catch them for him. But that was fine with me. I was just glad to get out and away from that creek and away from that scary big black bear."

About that time Joseph called Larry's name.

"You're up. If you are going to get a haircut today hop in the chair," Joseph said.

Rob asked TC, "Do you think you will go back fishing in that same spot?"

"No, I think I will stay away from there for a while," said TC. "There is one thing I learned from fishing rivers like that. You are the trespasser, the river belongs to the wild animals, and you best remember it. You know, there is one thing about colored hair. It sure doesn't take long to get a haircut."

In no time at all Larry was finished and we were ready to leave. All the men who were sitting in the barbershop got a big laugh out of watching us listening to TC's story. Joseph said, "You boys just come back anytime you want." We told him we sure would and thanks for the bubblegum and story. That was the good thing about getting haircuts when you are young; you always get a piece of bubblegum when you're finished.

CHAPTER 10

MRS. LINDA'S SECRETS

On the way back home they stopped by Jim's five-and-dime store to look at the new shipment of fireworks that just come in for the Fourth of July. This was a big deal for any ten-year-old boy to get to pop firecrackers by himself.

When they got back to Rob's house, Rob ran in to let Grandpa Paul know that the fireworks were in for the Fourth of July. Larry had to run home to help with the afternoon feeding. Rob asked, "Grandpa Paul are you going to let me pop the firecrackers by himself this year?"

Paul said, "Don't get your hopes up. I will just have to see how you do with the firecrackers, and how responsible you are. You could burn the whole place down if you're not careful."

"You know, while we are talking about fire, that Mrs. Linda when we went past her house today, there was smoke you could see for a long way off."

Rob said, "And by the way, she is a very strange lady. Larry and me thinks she must be making a potion of some kind."

"What?" Paul said.

Rob said, "Well, what happened to Bert? He is a full-grown dog, and his legs are only just three inches long. When he runs his belly drags on the ground.

Paul laughed and said, "Bert is a basset hound, his breed all look like that. And you leave Mrs. Linda alone. That poor woman has been through a lot. She lost her husband in the war and she just never got over it. You know she used to play professional baseball during the war. Most of the ballplayers was over fighting in the war so the team owners got women to play while the men were away. Well, that explains her rock throwing. You know she can still throw a rock pretty straight and hard for a lady her age. Rob said, "Well, she should, she was a pitcher and they said she was very good."

Paul said, "And she is still pretty good at it."

Rob spoke up and said, "Well, she doesn't need a shotgun as long as there are rocks around."

"I would go rabbit hunting with her any day," Rob said.

"The iron pot you seen her heating up, that is what she uses to make lye soap with," said Paul."

"OK, are we are still on strange?" Rob asked.

"What about the other day? She had a switch. And she was walking up and down her tomato rows, beating the ground around the plants."

Paul tried to explain to Rob. "She grew up in a time when people couldn't take a chance on not making a crop. They knew that the winter would be cold and long if they didn't have enough food to last through the whole winter, so they were very superstitious about everything. Now people were strange in those days, they would try anything," Paul said.

I don't know where or how switching the plants come to be, but I know a lot of people that still do that today.

"They believe it works," Paul said.

Rob said, "You just watch her tomatoes and see if it works or not."

"She may just make a believer out of you," Paul said.

"Well, her walking up and down the rows with that long elm switch was a little freighting, that made a believer out of me in itself."

Paul looked at Rob and said, "You don't have anything to worry about, she wouldn't harm a fly. You know every Sunday afternoon if it's not raining you can find her over at the cemetery. That's where her husband is buried. She will take a chair out there, sit down at his tombstone, and prop her feet up. You know she will sit there for hours and just talk to him, just like he is right there with her. You know to her he just may be. Sometimes she will read a book to him. She has been doing this for a year. That's how she deals with her loss. People have different ways of dealing with things that they face in their lives. When you lose someone close to you it seems like you can never feel that emptiness. When someone like that is gone you can never feel that empty hole that is left. Mrs. Linda is OK, she will do anything to help you. But you better stay out of her yard."

As time went on, me and Larry did get to pop our firecrackers. Grandpa Paul was very proud of us for not catching anything on fire. You know Mrs. Linda did have the prettiest tomatoes you have ever seen. Every tomato looked just like the other one. I was beginning to think there may just be something to that old superstition of switching the plants to make them grow. It sure seemed to work for Mrs. Linda.

It seemed like in no time at all the summer was about over, and school was going to be starting back. Grandma Lou took Rob into town to buy some clothes to start back to school in.

Rob asked Grandma, "Why are you buying everything so big?"

"You are a ten-year-old boy. Just wait a few mouths, they will be just fine," Lou said.

Rob went back to try on the new clothes. The shirts were all long sleeves and had to be turned up; the pants were too long and had to turn them up. And she had to buy me a belt, just to hold the pants up on my waist. Then my new shoes I had to stuff cotton in the toes to keep them from rubbing a blister on my back of my foot. Rob asked Grandma Lou, "This is just awful. Do I have to go back to school wearing these clothes?"

Lou just looked at Rob with a hard stare.

But you know when I started to go school most everyone looked just like me; their clothes were too big for them too. Grandma Lou was right; I and everyone else grew into all our clothes just fine by Christmas.

Even though Larry and Rob didn't go to the same school, they still made time to get together and play every chance they could get. Being raised on a farm was a lot of hard work in those days. A big family was something that was very popular. The more hands you had to work the farm, the easier it was on everyone. Some years are just better than others. You just take whatever you get and be thankful for what you have. Sometimes I wonder what makes a man want to be a farmer. You can work all year on something, taking the best care of it that you can, and an early frost can wipe it all out and thirty minutes. Farming gets in your blood, and when you start seeing the trees start blooming and grass start greening up, you forget all about what last year was like. So you get out there and start breaking ground.

You know farming isn't much different than raising kids, a little bit of good, rich, fertile ground. A little water and a lot of patience, and the kids and the crops will grow off just fine. That is what Paul always said.

When you have that year when everything goes well for you, you better put a little something back. Also you better enjoy it because you can bet next year will be different.

CHAPTER 11

SUMMER OVER SCHOOL STARTING AGAIN

Grandma Lou got all the clothes home and gave them a good washing before the first day of school. Rob was still complaining to Grandpa Paul about how big they fit on him.

"Just wait a minute, Rob, your Grandma Lou knows what she talking about. She raised your dad, he came out just fine. He may have had a few bumps and bruises along the way, but when he hit the ground he bounced OK. Just do what she says and quit complaining."

It was Friday and school was to start on Monday morning. Rob was not at all looking forward to going to school without his best friend Larry by his side. This would be his first day going to this new school at Cutter's Crossing. But there would be weekends and a little bit of time after school. That was until the days started getting shorter; Rob would be busy after school each day helping Grandpa Paul with feeding and taking care of all the livestock.

It wasn't long and then it was Monday, and Lou had Rob up early to catch the school bus. It ran at 7:00 a.m. If you were not out there at 7:00 a.m. the bus driver would just pass you up and never even slow down, honk, wave, or anything. So 7:01 a.m. you missed it. You would have to find you another ride to school for that day.

Lou was running around getting everything ready for Rob when she heard the bus coming down the old gravel road. Lou jumped and ran over to toward the table grabbed Rob by the back of his shirt and took off for the kitchen door almost dragging Rob all the way down the driveway. Lou had Rob's shirt nearly pulled over his head with one hand by the time they got to the driveway. The other hand she had a flapjack trying to cram it in Rob's mouth. The bus came to a stop just as Lou and Rob got to the bus door.

The bus driver opened the door and looked at Rob, and Lou Rob had a mouth full of flapjacks and couldn't say a word. He wanted to introduce himself to them. Mr. Gregory looked at Lou; she was still in her house coat and what looked like a head scarf tied around some rollers she had in her hair. He looked at Rob again; Rob still couldn't say a word because of the mouthful of flapjacks. "My name is Shorty Gregory," he said.

Right away it was pretty clear why the called him Shorty. Mr. Gregory wasn't even as tall as a third grader. Rob said hi and started up the steps and went in to find a seat. Mr. Gregory told Lou, "I will have him home at 3:45 p.m. sharp."

Rob sat down on the right side of the bus close to Mr. Gregory. That's when he noticed that Mr. Gregory had blocks of wood tied to his paddles so he could reach them with his feet because his legs was so short. He had a walking cane hanging on the lever that opened the front door. That way he could open and close the door without getting out of the driver's seat every time he pulled to a bus stop to pick up more kids. It was the most amazing thing you have ever seen. Mr. Gregory was about in his late sixties. He didn't have a tooth in his head. He was a very jolly man and was always laughing so you could always see in his mouth; there was not a single tooth in his head. All you could see was smooth, pretty pink gums top and bottom.

He wore a straw hat and overalls every day. He wore a pair of black work boots that had real tall soles on them. I guess he thought it would make him look bigger. It didn't help it just made him walk funny. It looked like he walked stiff legged like he had something wrong with him. Mr. Gregory was light on his feet, and could move around like a young man. He had a nickname for everyone on the bus. He could not remember anyone's real name. You know that didn't make any sense to Rob how he could not remember their names and be able to remember their nicknames for everyone. You know every day as soon as they got on the bus he always would greeted them with a hello and then their nickname.

There was one little girl that lived up to the road name Gloria. He called her morning glory; well, he almost got hers right every day. He called me Tater, never knew where he come up with that name from or anyone else's, but it sure was interesting. The bus ride to school was quite not much talking; everyone had to get up early so they were still trying to wake up before they would get to school. But then the ride home was so loud you could hardly talk to person sitting right next to you.

When we got to school that morning, all the teachers was out by the bus stop in front school with clipboards in there hands. My teacher was the one with the funny tall paper hat; it had the grade written on it that I was going into. That made it easy for the newcomer to find out where they needed to go. On the clipboard it was listed with everyone's name that was in their class. All you had to know was what class you would be going into. And then look at the list and find your name then you would know who would be your teacher. Rob would be going into the fifth grade because he would be turning eleven years old this year.

This was going to be his first year at Cutter's Crossing School. He hadn't got a chance to meet a lot of boys his age, only Mickey Jones and Joey Green. They were going to be in the sixth grade, and he knew he would miss his best friend Larry who went over to the Pine Ridge Color School out south of town.

My teacher's name was Mrs. Mitchell; she was a middle-aged woman who was old enough to have gray hair but didn't have one gray hair on her head. She was a tall and thin lady who made her face and neck look real long, and her nose was long and slim and came to point, really unusually long for a normal person. But she was a very happy lady and loved being a teacher; she had a lot of energy and full of ideas that would make teaching a lot of fun.

When she got everyone together, they went inside down a long hallway to the end of hall, and that was where our classroom was. When we went in, her classroom was fixed up with a lot of pictures from all around the different places in the world. My first thought was it looked like geography was going to be a big deal this year. This was a lot different from the classroom up north and a lot less students in each classroom. With only twenty-six students in the class everything should be a lot more fun.

Without knowing any of the boys in the classroom, I didn't really know how to get to know them. But as soon as we all sat down in our chairs Mrs. Mitchell had everyone stand up and tell who they were and where they lived.

After that, Mrs. Mitchell said, "It was time for us to go out to the playground for a few minutes, for playtime. This gave everyone time to get all the wiggles out and meet the new kids who were there for the first time. Rob noticed one thing about country kids that was different from city kids: it was that country kids were a lot more fun, happy. Paul says living in the country takes a lot of pressure off day-to-day struggles and a lot less worries for the parents and the kids. One thing about it, no one had any stress in those days around Cutter's Crossing. Everyone were farmers, and they were all in the about the same shape.

The first day of school was over before Rob knew it, and it was time to catch the bus to go back home. Grandma Lou was waiting at the driveway when the bus came pulling up. Shorty Gregory, the bus driver, opened the door and said, "Mrs. Lou, I told you I will have him home at three forty-five sharp. Lou looked at her watch on her arm. It was exactly three forty-five p.m. Rob stepped off the bus, and Lou said, "Thank you, see you in the morning." Mr. Shorty closed the door and drove off down the road.

Rob ran through the front door dropped his things, and ran out the back door to help Paul in the barn. Paul asked, "How was the first day of school?"

Rob said, "This was going to be a fun year. Everyone in the class was a lot of fun, and Mrs. Mitchell was very excited about what we were going to do and learn this year and looked like learning was going to fun. Mrs. Mitchell said that we had a field trip planned for later this year to the state capital," Rob said with excitement.

Lou had cooked Rob's favorite dish for supper since it was his first day at school. Paul and Rob had all the feeding all finished, and now they were headed to the back door. Rob got a whiff of those fried potatoes and right in the middle of a sentence Paul looked at him, and he took off at an all-out hard run for the back door. Paul just shook his head and thought to himself, since there was no one there to talk to, I guess he had worked up an appetite at school. Lou she just loved to cook for Rob.

After supper they sat at the kitchen table for a while and listened to Rob talk about his day. "Sounds like you are making friends," Lou said then Paul spoke up and said, with a big smile on his face, "Let's go and see what's on the TV set before bath time. Rob, you are going to have to go to bed earlier. I've seen you and Lou running around the kitchen and almost missed the bus, and Lou you may want to button your house coat all the way up if you're going to sprint to the bus stop with Rob every morning."

CHAPTER 12

RABBIT HUNTING DOWN AT THE RIVER BOTTOMS

After getting the first-day jitters out of the way, now catching the bus became a regular routine. After that morning it became a lot easier with no drama. The school year went by fast; in no time at all it was Christmas, and we were out for two weeks. Rob hadn't had much time to play with Larry and missed him very much. As soon as school was out on Friday, Rob and Larry had planned a hunting trip to go hunting for rabbits. They were hoping for snow, which would make it a lot easier to find them, since they didn't have a dog to hunt with. A good cold day and the white snow covered landscape and all you would have to do, would be to look for the rabbit's breath to rise up out of the snow. The old rabbit couldn't run very fast in deep snow. That would make it a lot easier to get them. But on this morning it was cool and no snow.

They got up early on Saturday morning and rode their bikes down to the river levy. They were a lot of brush and cover for the rabbits to hide from other animals that could catch them. All Rob and Larry had were slingshots and marbles that they liked to use, to hunt with. Larry and Rob were crack shots with the slingshots that Paul had made each of them. When they got down to the levy, it was about 9:00 a.m. They saw Mickey Jones from the sixth-grade class. He had already got his Christmas present from Santa early. It was a pellet gun that shot little round lead balls. He had been trying to shoot a rabbit for the last two hours and had not hit one yet. About that time one came out from under some brush close to them. Larry loaded up a marble in one second; he had hit the rabbit. Mickey was very surprised. "Hey, Larry, can I try that?" Mickey said. Then another one came out behind them. Rob loaded up and shot and down went the rabbit.

Mickey left the pellet gun with the bikes and walked on up the levy with both the boys. Within an hour they had two rabbits each and were ready to go back home. Paul had taught the boys never take more than what they needed, and that there will always be food when anyone needed it. These two rabbits will make a big pot of rabbit stew that they could eat on for maybe two days.

When they got back to the bikes, Mickey let them shoot the pellet gun. Rob had found an old bucket in a junk pile that someone had made. It looked like the trash dumped there was trash that someone didn't need from around their house. This made the area around the river bottoms look bad, but regularly someone from the county would look through the trash for someone's name. If they found a name somewhere in the trash, the person that was responsible for the trash would have to come in clean all of it up then would have to pay a fine for dumping it.

After getting the rabbits home, Grandma Lou told Rob he better get to dress the rabbits and get them real good and clean if you want them cook for supper. They hadn't had rabbit stew in a while; Paul said, "This was like old" times. If you pour you out a big bowl of rabbit stew with some of Lou's fresh hot corn bread and add a big glass of buttermilk, it makes me feel just how lucky I am to be living in a place where you can still go out and hunt for your own food. Like my father had to do so many time for all of us kids. Back in those days rabbits and squirrels were hunted by everyone. They were not very many so when you brought one home it was a treat for everyone.

After supper it was Saturday night. Jackie Gleason show came on at seven thirty; it was a lot of fun to see that loudmouth bus driver from the city. His wife's name was Alice. That Jackie Gleason was always hollering at her about something. And his neighbors Ed and Trixy, this made Paul laugh so loud you could hear him all the way at the barn. Grandma Lou said, "Tomorrow is Sunday we have to get to church early if you want to get a good seat up front. Rob, you need to get up and get your breakfast. You can't be lying in the bed just because you have a day off." Paul and Lou always liked to set up front on the second row back on the right side. It was kind of strange how people always set in the same spot every Sunday morning. Sure made it easier to know when someone was missing. All you had to do is look for an empty place in the pew.

The first Sunday morning of every month was potluck dinner. I always wonder why they called it potluck. Sometimes the food looked really good. But sometimes it was really bad. I guess that was the luck part; you never knew what it was going to taste like, if you didn't know who cooked it. You always wanted to be there when the ladies were bringing their food in so you could see who brought what. And hope that there weren't many pots and pans that were the same color. That could really mess you up when you was going down the line to fill up your plate. One trip was about all you would get. If you thought you were going to get seconds, you better think again. By the time everyone went through, everything was pretty much all gone if it was any good. What was left you did want seconds on. Paul would say there is a reason why it is left; don't even try it.

Clare Bell's pots or pans were always the first ones that were empty. She was a German lady that lived out east of town who had an apple orchard. She also always grew sweet potatoes ever year. She once had the best sweet potatoes in the whole state and was invited to the state capital for a farmers' meeting with John, the local county agent. She got to tell everyone in the state how she grew the potatoes that year. And they were very surprised when they heard just how she did it.

She is a very old-fashioned lady and still practiced old ways and was very superstitions. Just like Mrs. Linda and her tomato plants, she also would take an elm switch and walk up and down her rows if she had a row that wasn't doing as good as the rest. She would get to whipping the ground around the plant and threaten the plant if it didn't get to growing there would be more where that came from.

They said the man from the state thought all that was not normal. It just wasn't a good practice of today's farming, but he couldn't argue with her old ways. It seemed to work for her. She was most likely the best cook in the whole county. She could open a restaurant and just serve fried chicken, nothing else.

If you had ever tasted her fried chicken, you never would forget it. I think people would keep her so busy, she wouldn't have time to do anything else but cook chicken every day.

Grandma Lou was excited about a new recipe she had made for Sunday dinner. It was a three-bean casserole; Paul said, "Sure sound like a fancy word for a pot of beans." Grandma Lou looked at Paul and said, "The cooking magazine I got it from called it a casserole, so that's what we are going to call it."

It was very good and didn't last long and the pan was empty. It was very pretty, had a lot of colors to it. Rob thought to himself, It sure was a shame to see someone take the first spoonful out of it. But you know that made Grandma Lou feels good that everyone liked her new dish from that fancy magazine. A lot of the ladies who knew she had brought it were asking for the recipe so they could make for them self at home. Paul looked at Lou and told her that her fancy pot of beans was very good, and then Paul gave her a wink from his left eye.

One thing for sure was, Rob saw words how a small town church here in Cutter's Crossing had so many caring people. Everyone went to that church most of their lives. They grew close to each other just as if they were all family. It didn't take long, and Rob had bonded with everyone there. They took him in that church the same as if he had lived there his whole life.

CHAPTER 13

❧

CLASSROOM PLAY

It was a long afternoon, and it was very busy after they got back home with all the feeding to do. But it was good quality time once a month with the church family. The next day was Monday, and it was back to school. This would not be a late TV night. Grandma Lou said, "Rob, you better get to bed early. I will only holler at you once." I never knew why she always said that. Lou started hollering from the time the alarm went off till the bus came. Paul learned to get up and get out to the barn for the morning feeding till breakfast was ready. That was when he would come back in the house. Lou was always calmed down by then.

Well, Monday morning came. When we got to school, Mrs. Mitchell was excited about getting the classroom play together.

This was the time of the year that we would have to put on the play for the whole school. We would have to learn it before school would be out for the summer. This was a big deal and would be very embarrassing for some of us who didn't want to be in the play anyway. But Mrs. Mitchell would not take no from anyone; she said everyone would have a part. There would be something for them. If nothing else they could be what she called a prop. Rob thought maybe Mrs. Mitchell would let me be a tree, or a log maybe something like that. Being a tree all I would have to do is know where to stand because trees don't talk. So Rob thought he would not have to learn any lines.

Well, that wasn't going to happen since Rob was one of the smartest in the class. He probably had the most imagination of anyone in the whole classroom. Everyone liked him; he wasn't the class clown, but he did his part of making people laugh when he had a chance. Mrs. Mitchell handed out parts to those who she wanted to play what. Mrs. Mitchell said, "We will be trying out in two weeks for the part you have. If you don't want to play the part that I gave you, this will be a good time to trade with someone else. Otherwise, learn you part and be ready in two weeks for trying out the part you have."

Well, with twelve weeks until school was out, Mrs. Mitchell said that we will have six weeks to learn our parts. We all looked over our parts, and the play would be about famous fables. My part was about John Henry. He was a steel-driving man who worked on the railroad. Mrs. Mitchell knew what she was doing with this play. It gave each person a chance to learn about someone famous in history and what they did and how their lives played an important part in history.

Mrs. Mitchell was a great teacher and made learning a lot of fun. It looked like this would be a lot of fun for everyone. After learning the play, everyone in classroom would learn a little something about all the famous people in history. Except for Mary Ann Stevens, Mrs. Mitchell gave her a part that didn't make any sense. Mary Ann was going to be Mother Teresa, no one could figure that one out. She was about the biggest tomboy in fifth-grade class. She could kick a football farther than any boy in the fifth- or sixth-grade class. She wasn't that big but very strong and tough. None of the boys liked her. She could throw a perfect spiral too. Farther then any boy in the fifth or sixth grade, but she didn't care if they liked her or not. She knew she could beat them up any day they wanted to try her.

She had four other sisters and only one brother, which didn't make any sense. Her sisters were about as girly as they could be. Her brother, he was a lot older by six years but very athletic, fast, and very good at football and baseball. I think she missed it somewhere and should have been a boy. But she was the prettiest thing you had ever seen. She had long dark-brown hair and the prettiest dark eyes I have ever seen on a girl before.

None of it made any sense. Now Mrs. Mitchell wanted Mary Ann to play Mother Teresa in the class play. Rob thought now this was going to be interesting.

Lucky for me, Mrs. Mitchell had a lot of books in her classroom library. And she had one about John Henry. I got to take it home to read up on Mr. John Henry. I found out that he was a very strong black man who worked for the railroad. This man was perfect for me since my best friend was a black boy name Larry. This made Rob miss Larry, and he couldn't wait until weekend so he could tell him about John Henry.

That afternoon when Rob got home he told Grandma Lou about the class play that they would be putting on in six weeks. Rob said he was going to be playing John Henry.

Rob was very excited about that, then he asked Grandma Lou if she could make a costume for him to wear in the play. Rob told Grandma Lou he would have to stand up in front of everyone and tell a few things about John Henry and how important his life was. How his hard work made it possible for people to travel across county by train. This was the best and fastest way to travel in those days.

As the weeks went by the play became more interesting for the entire students. Mrs. Mitchell was right; we all learn a lot about so many different famous people because of what they did; their life changed things in history. Now we would have things in us that we would never forget for the rest of our lives.

CHAPTER 14

PREACHING ON THE
STREET CORNER

The school year went by so fast, and it was time for summer break. This was a busy time for the farmers and their families, now with spring planting getting here. Everything had to be ready to be put in the ground. The first part of summer break was all about hard work. If you had a Grandpa like Paul, he worked so hard and fast for an old man in his late sixties. He didn't look back to see if whoever was working with him was keeping up or not. So by the end of the day, Rob was very tired and Grandma Lou didn't never have to tell him to get cleaned up and ready for bed. Rob knew that the next day would be another day like that one. Until everything was in the ground, which was when he would be able to play with Larry and catch up on everything that they liked to do.

It was hard to believe that fifth grade was over and Rob would be starting in the sixth grade in the fall. Rob would be turning twelve years old by middle of summer and getting to be a big kid and becoming to be a lot of help for Paul and Lou.

Joe, Rob's father, knew what he was doing leaving Rob with Paul and Lou. That was one thing that Joe learned from Paul, when he was growing up and that was how to work, the automobile plant where Joe worked up in the city. You know it didn't take long when the management saw what kind of worker Joe was, he was a very dependable employee. Joe learned that at a very young age, if you had something to do, you need to get up and kick the covers off of you and hit the floor. If not the work may never get done. The management in that big automobile plant, promoted Joe to head shift supervisor in a very short time. Paul was a good teacher and had a lot of patience. He took the time to show Rob how things worked as well as how things were done. Paul did the same with Joe.

Joe knew he would be a good teacher for Rob. One thing that Joe loved most about his father is that he would be a good teacher for Rob. It was important to not only work, but don't let the work beat you down. There were always other ways that were easier ways to do things if you stop, slow down, think about what you are doing. Paul always said he had old ways of doing things and said he always like to do things the hard way. But the truth was Paul was one of the most amazing people you would ever meet.

But if you ever worked with Paul for any time or reason, you could see in a short time just what kind of a person he really was. Full of wisdom and knowledge, it seemed like he could figure out about anything if he would put his mind to it. Joe was just like Paul, the older he got. Joe was as strong and quick as anyone his age. The big factory was always giving him extra paychecks and sending him on trips all over the country just for some of his ideas and suggestions that Joe would tell them, and it would save the factory lots of money. This would make everyone's jobs a lot easier and run a lot smoother.

Rob asked Paul if he could take Saturday afternoon off to play with Larry. So Rob went out to get his bike and rode over to Larry's house. On the way over to Larry's house he went across the White Oak Creek. And looked over the side and saw that gypsies were camped out down by the creek. They were in a bus and had a big white tent set up close to the water.

So he rode on faster so he could to get Larry so they could come back to see what they were up to. Sometimes they would go around town and play guitars and sing on the corner preaching the gospel and handing out flyers. This would make for an interesting afternoon. No one knew where they came from or how long they would stay, or where they would go from here. The women would always have on long dresses that dragged on the ground when they walked with long sleeves down to their hands with the top button of their dress tied to their neck, no matter how hot it was. Their hair I guess they never cut it, because it would be down to the bend of their legs. But they were some of the best singers you would have ever heard anywhere, even on the radio.

The men always wore a nice dark suit and tie with a hat on their head. After they sang and played a few songs, one of the men would start talking. It would be a little like the auctioneer over at the sale barn, where the livestock are sold, talking real loud, and with a very strong voice. The only difference in him and the auctioneer is everyone could clearly understand the men very well, but he could talk just as fast. Then the oddest thing would happen. He would start crying like a nine-year-old boy. Tears would roll down his face and drop on the sidewalk. By this time there would be a large crowd. Sometimes people would step out and go to them, and one of the men would put his hands on them and start calling out to Jesus with a loud voice. Then before long they would both be crying. This was a little different than the way everyone worshiped out at our Baptist Church. Out at the church where Lou and Paul and I went, I wonder what would happen if they were to come in talk to all of us like they do down on the street corner. This could be very interesting on what could happen. It sure was something how the two men and the two ladies looked like they were about the happiest people you would ever want to meet. They would always smile at everyone the whole time they were talking to them. This made for an interesting and fun-filled afternoon. Larry and Rob sat there on their bikes and watched until all the people started to leave and the people started to calm down.

This was pretty common in this area in the early sixties for people to go from town to town like this. Some people would call them Holly roller, I never knew just what people meant by those remarks. They really seemed like very loving and caring people and would never cause any kind of trouble of any kind.

CHAPTER 15

LEARNING TO BE COUNTY AGENTS

It was hard to believe the summer was going by so fast. Rob and Larry spent a lot of time working for Larry's father to help with his pig farm like giving a helping hand. Meanwhile, Paul was stuck with the farming. It seemed like there was just not enough time in a day to get everything done. Rob and Larry were growing up fast and were becoming very strong for boys their age. Grandma Lou said they were from good stock. The best thing about these two boys was their willingness to work without complaining. They never knew any other way; that was the way Paul wanted to teach Rob. Sometimes it was interesting to work with Paul; he made sure he took the time to explain how to do things. This always made working with him go a lot more smoothly and without confusion. The one thing you could bet on was with Paul, any confusion and Paul would throw up his hands, and you would go to what he would call training 101 until you understood what you were doing and could do it right.

At the end of the afternoon or about four o'clock, Rob and Larry were off for the day; most of the time they would go down to clear fork for a swim before supper to cool off. They would have to be careful at that time of the day, you never knew who would be there swimming. Some of the older teenage boys in the area didn't like swimming with black people, and if Rob and Larry were swimming there at that time, they would leave real fast, or there could be trouble when they saw Larry. If someone was already there they would just stay on their bikes and keep riding right on by, and come back another day. It sure was good to have a place to swim so close to the house.

The next day, John the county agent asked Paul and, Larry's father if he could use the two boys to help him pull some sample of Paul's corn on the back fifteen acres. This was his winter feed corn for his livestock, partly and the rest to sell. He wanted to know if he needed to spray something on the corn before it started to make ears.

That John, he was always trying to encourage any of the young kids around the valley to become farmers. They were the valley's future farmers, and it was important to make sure they knew that, and one day the valley would be counting on them to step up and take their place as farmers. John wanted them to learn how to look for problems with all their crops. They would need to cut, pull, and gather a few boxes of corn stocks to take back to John's office so he could look over the samples closely. John said, "Boys, this may take most of the day." John stopped by Polly's and picked up some sandwiches and crackers and a gallon of sweet tea to take back to the office. John got bologna with cheese, mayo, lettuce, and a big tomato. Larry got chicken loaf, with mustard and sweet pickle. Rob got bacon loaf cheese, tomato, mustard. John said, "You can't beat that

Petty Jean lunch meat anywhere in the state. You boys better get all you want."

It was all business when John dumped the corn samples out on a big table in the back of his offices. John asked Larry to get some glass jars with lids from the cabinets. "OK, boys, look though the stocks to see if you see any insects crawling around. That's the first thing we need to do. I sure don't want any bugs crawling around in my office."

We found a few small insects called mayflies. "Not too much to worry about," John said. So John took some over to a machine to run the stocks through. It mashed and chopped them up so he could look at the fibers inside of the stock. He never tried to explain just what he was doing, so we just watched, and we didn't have any questions. It was sure good to have a man like John that lived here in the valley to watch out for all the farmers in our area. We just can't let an infestation of insects or something like that get started here. "If you let them go this year, next year will be a lot worse," John said. This was an interesting day. Rob and Larry learned a lot. They knew what to look for when it came to farming corn.

Time passed and it wasn't long and it was time for school to start again. There wase still talk of closing the black school down and putting them with the whites in public school. Most of the people were OK with that, but they were still a few people who were not so happy about it. But time would tell; it looked like it was going to happen. But not likely going to happen this year.

Our president, Lynden B. Johnson, of this great nation is working on equal rights for all of the black people. This is now 1965, and the black people were now starting to get equal rights even in Cutter's Crossing. So Larry went back to his school and Rob went to his. They still made time to get together on weekends to catch up on play time. One thing was that these two boys were very close bonded with a friendship that would stand up to about anything. They were so much rooted in Cutter's Crossing just like a lot of other close friends and family.

Delbert's story time

CHAPTER 16

COOLING UNDER THE WALNUT TREE

It was a very hot day, and the two boys had been so busy that it was never enough time to play like they used to. Rob would like to go over to Larry's house and play baseball with him and his brothers. They always liked to let Rob pitch. It was hard to believe that a twelve-year-old boy like Rob could throw as hard as someone who was seventeen or eighteen years old. Rob could throw a curve ball that would break so much that Larry's brother couldn't hit the ball unless Rob would let him. Larry would always play back catcher. The two boys made a great team and loved playing baseball together. Rob was strong and built like his dad, Joe. Larry was fast and as quick as anyone you have ever seen, all those years of chasing the little pigs around the pigpen to separate them for his dad. It must have worked for Larry, he was as quick as a cat.

It was Saturday morning, and Rob and Larry rode their bikes to town. They rode by the big walnut tree. It was a hot day, and at least four or five men were sitting on a bench under the old walnut tree where they would stop and talk. They were all retired men and very interesting. All they had to do was sit and talk about old times. One man named Virgil May was one of the quietest of the whole bunch. There would always be a pile of pine shavings that would go up to his knees. He would carve lots of little figures of animals that looked very detailed and lifelike. Frankie Jones was an old man who was a war hero from World War II. Frankie was full of stories about Germany. One day they told of a time he and his platoon was pinned down in foxholes and ran out of ammo. He had to fight ten men off with his bare hands. He was a big man and still looked strong for an older man in his late fifties. He still stood up straight like a young man. One time he had a slight limp on his left side where he got wounded in the war. He now raises cattle north of town. So no one disagreed with him about anything he would say.

We liked to sit down and listen to what he would tell us about what it was like for those young men fighting for our great nation. He would get real tense at times when he would talk about things that went on. He would have a blank stare without ever blinking an eye. His facial expression would change, so you could tell by looking that he would be right back in that foxhole again fighting those men. It was times like this that all the other men would stop talking and listen to old Frankie. They knew he just needed to get it out so he could deal with what had happened to him. Wouldn't take long, and he would snap back to himself, and all would be back to normal with all laughing and joking as usual.

One of the other men, Holly Gene Rackley, always carried buckeyes in his pocket and liked to give them away to everyone that he would see. He would say, "Here, carry this buckeye in your pocket every day, and don't forget that it will bring you good fortune. When you put on your pants every morning, let that be the first thing you put in your pocket."

I asked him what good fortune meant. Holly Gene would say, "It don't always mean money."

He would say, "There is a lot more to having good fortune than just money, good health, good friends, and good family."

He would say that with a smile. I think he really understood what that meant and wanted everyone else to understand it like he did.

Time would pass so fast. There would be so many tales that were being told, we didn't won't to get up and leave in the middle of a story. We could easily have spent hours sitting under that old walnut tree learning about how it was for those old men growing up like they did. These men were clearly the roots of this small town called Cutter's Crossing. I felt very proud that I could grow up with men like this. They had been through the worst of times and the best of times. Their faith in who was really in control of everything made me realize that I could count on any one of them if I needed them at any time.

CHAPTER 17

LITTLE JOHN'S FISHING TIPS

Larry looked at me and said, "We have got to get down to the co-op to find the big hooks we need to fish with." They jumped on their bikes and took off to the co-op down the street, pulled up on the sidewalk next to the door, and jumped off their bikes before ever coming to a stop. The bikes bounced off the wall next to a big plate window at the front of the store. They ran inside back to where the fishing tackle was. Jackie Smith and his wife were the owners of the co-op. Jackie meet Rob and Larry at the back of the store and showed them all the hooks he had. Joe Green came in and needed help finding hinges for a gate he was putting on his barn, and Jackie had to go help him. Little John and his pet pig, Missy, was in the back waiting to pick up a load of feed for his pigs when he saw Larry and Rob looking at the fishing tackle.

Little John and Missy walked up and asked the two boys what they were looking for. Larry spoke up and said, "Hooks for catfish." Mickey Jones had been catching a lot of flathead cats down in the White Oak, and some were ten pounders.

Little John said, "Boys, you don't need fish hooks to catch big catfish. Rob, has your grandpa Paul not taken you noodling yet?"

Rob said, "What is noodling?"

Little John said, "It's easier than fishing, because those big catfish like to lay in holes under the water next to the creek bank. All you have to do is jump in the water, find those holes in the banks of the creek, and stick your hand in the hole until you feel a catfish. It will most likely bite down on your hand. That's when you just pull him out, and you better be ready to hand him off to someone else. You're going to want to turn him loose."

Larry looked at Rob and Rob looked back at Larry. Larry's eyes were big as half dollars. He didn't look like he thought it would be something he would want to do. Little John said, "What's the matter, boys, it's fun. You should try it!"

"Well, we may need to think about that. It sounds a little bit dangerous."

"Boys, I'll take you. It will be fun. Those big catfish are just lying back in those big holes, and they won't bite anything you throw at them, that's why you can't catch them. They just wait until a little fish swims by and then jumps out and gets it. That's the only way you going to catch them in to and drag them out."

Little John did take us noodling, and he was right; it was about the most fun we had ever had. It was something to see a grown man in is late sixties jump into the water and wade down the creek bank and pull out fifteen-pound catfish out with his bare hand. He could get around like a man in his twenties as strong and as light on his feet as one.

This was something Rob and Larry would not ever forget about Little John; that man would take time away from his busy day and spend it with neighborhood kids.

"Well, how about frog gigging? I have a ten-foot gig pole in my truck you two can take with you. Go over to Frankie Jones's stock pond. I've seen lots of frogs in there the other night when my dog and Missy were coon hunting in the woods behind the pond. All you need is a burlap sack and a good bright flashlight. One of you holds the light on the frog while the other gigs him. I will give y'all six bits for a dozen big frog legs."

"Thanks, Little John," Rob said. "Sounds like something we may want to try out. We would like to take you up on that gig pole."

Rob and Larry met Little John at his truck where he handed them the pole. "Thanks, Little John."

They got on their bikes and headed to home. Larry had to go on home and get all his chores done if he was going to go frog gigging after dark. Rob jumped off his bike and took the gig to the barn and showed Grandpa Paul and told him what Little John had said. "That sounds good. I don't think anyone could make those frog legs taste any better than your Grandma Lou. I haven't had any frog legs in a while."

Paul said, "I will hunt you boys a burlap sack for tonight, and I will let ya'll use my good flashlight if you take care of it and don't lose it."

After supper Larry came over about dark. The boys gathered up things and headed over to Frankie Jones's house. Grandma Lou called and talked to Suzanne, Frankie's wife, about the boys coming over to frog gig in their stock pond. Lou got them permission.

It was about eight thirty at night and just got good and dark when they got to Frankie's meadow where the stock pond was. Larry and Rob crossed over to the fence and started to the pond. The moon was barely shining, and without the flashlight that Grandpa Paul let them take, they wouldn't be able to find the stock pond. They started over a hill in the field and were almost to the pond when they heard something running toward them, but they couldn't see what it was. Larry was carrying the flashlight and started running back to the fence where they came in. That left Rob carrying the frog gig. He looked back, and there was no way he would ever catch up with Larry, but he was going to try. That's when the source of the noise they were hearing came out to where Rob could see it. It was Frankie's Big Jersey bull. One thing that made Jersey bulls different from other bulls was that they were a lot meaner and more protective of their cows. Suzanne forgot to tell Grandma Lou about the Jersey bull in the pasture and for some reason forgot to tell Rob and Larry. Larry easily made it back to the fence and was already on the other side looking at Rob running back toward him as fast as he could go. Rob had already dropped the big frog gig pole. Larry was shining the flashlight in the bull's eyes to try to slow him down enough so Rob could make it over the fence. That bull was just inches from Rob's heels as he got close to the fence. Larry yelled, "Slide!"

That's when Rob slid down where Larry was holding up the bottom wire of the fence as high as he could to give all the room for Rob to slide under. It looked like that would be his only hope to get away from the bull. It was just Rob's luck. He had made it under the fence without a scratch when the old bull gave a big snort and stomped his feet and went running back to his cows. Larry looked at Rob and asked, "What happened to the gig pole?"

"I think it's somewhere between here and the stock pond. Sorry, Larry, I think I'm ready to call it a night, unless you want to go in and try to find the gig yourself."

"Nope", Larry said, "I think this was enough excitement from me. We can come back in the morning and get the gig."

"I agree," Rob said. "Let's go back home."

When they got home it was only about nine fifteen, and Lou said, "Well, how many you catch? It sure didn't take ya'll long."

"Sorry, Grandma. We were chased out the pasture by Frankie's Jersey bull. He was a mean one. We will have to go back in the morning to get the gig 'cause I left it laying somewhere in the pasture."

The next morning they went to see if they could find the gig. Luckily for them all the cows were out at the other end of the pasture, so Rob and Larry found the gig in no time, and they were on their way back home. This worked out good for Rob and Larry. They went frog gigging many more times, but one thing they did was to check out the pastures and stock ponds before they went at night.

Summertime passed fast, and it was already time to start junior high. This was going to be a big deal for both of the boys because the colored school was closing down, and they were coming to Cutter's Crossing High School. Rob and Larry and a lot of others were very excited also.

CHAPTER 18

SCHOOL CONSOLIDATION

Just before the end of the school year was over, all the colored kids had to be bussed two counties away because none of the schools would take them in the area. They would have to catch the bus before 6:00 a.m., and wouldn't get home until 6:00 p.m. The principal from the colored school went to the high school at Cutter's Crossing and asked if school would take them into school. They agreed and all was set for them to start this school year. The summer went by really fast and school was going to start on Monday.

Tension was high that morning when the school bus loaded with the colored kids pulled up in front of the school. A lot of people had gathered out at the bus stop to see the colored kids get off the bus. All the white kids got off the bus first except Rob. All the black kids were picked up first and were loaded on the back of the bus. Rob didn't know what to expect when all the colored kids started getting off the bus, so he decided to stay on the bus and get off when they did. Rob wanted to be sure there wouldn't be any trouble.

When all the kids got off the bus they had, a lost look on their faces and seemed very misplaced. Larry had slipped over by some of his family and friends where he felt more conformable. Rob walked over to Larry and grabbed his shoulder and said, "Let's go into our classroom. I will show you and the others where to go."

That's when Gloria Smith stepped forward where the girls were standing when they got off the bus, and said, "Welcome to our school. My name is Gloria Smith. All eighth graders follow me and I will show you to your class. I will take the rest of you to the office and someone will get you to your class."

The principal, Mr. Bruce Lester, stepped outside and was very pleased with Larry and Gloria and how they had helped these scared little colored kids. By the look on their faces he could tell they didn't know what to expect. He spoke up and took charge and made the rest of them feel welcome. In a matter of minutes everyone was headed to their classes. Mr. Lester thought about how he would feel if he had been in their shoes. He wanted them to feel welcome and be accepted. This was going to be a permanent move for them, and he wanted nothing but a smooth transition. He was so glad to be part of this time in history, and live in a town like Cutter's Crossing where they had kids like Rob and Gloria in his school.

Time went on as the school year started, and everyone was accepted. The football coach found out how fast Larry was and wanted him to go out for football. He already knew about Rob and how strong he was. He knew how fast he could throw a baseball, and thought he should be able to throw a football as well. He was right. Rob could throw a football one hundred yards, and Larry could run so fast he could be down there to catch anything Rob could throw at him. Larry became the first colored to play on the school's football team. The next year a lot of the others joined in and played sports. Basketball and football turned out real well the next year. The high school won the state championship! Everyone was excited for the school and how all the kids joined together.

ABOUT THE AUTHOR

I was born on a small farm near a town in Central Arkansas. Families depended on each other; that was just the way we were and how we were raised. I was one of thirteen children, eight boys and five girls. Mom and Dad had their hands full trying to feed and take care of all of us. We all had to do our part in taking care of each other and helping out Mom and Dad in any way we could. There was never a time when we didn't have anything to do. We loved summertime when school was out. We had other neighborhood kids who lived all around us to play with.

We had a very loving and caring family. We grew up poor and had poor ways of doing things. I still practice those ways today. I have a son who was twenty-four years old when my daughter was born. I hope they can grow up and see the importance of close family as I did. The older I got the more I realized how deeply rooted I was in that small town. How people whom I grew up with became very important in my life. I will never forget close friends whom I grew up and played with. My brothers and I still have a bond that will last us the rest of our lives.

CPSIA information can be obtained
at www.ICGtesting.com
Printed in the USA
FFOW04n0929020717
37299FF